MEET THE GIRL TALK CHARACTERS

Sabrina Wells is petite, with curly auburn hair, sparkling hazel eyes, and a bubbly personality. Sabrina loves magazines, shopping, sleepovers, and most of all, she loves talking to her best friends.

Katie Campbell is a straight-A student and super athlete. With her blond hair, blue eyes, and matching clothes, she's everyone's idea of little miss perfect. But Katie has a few surprises for everyone, including herself!

Randy Zak has just moved to Acorn Falls from New York City, and is she ever cool! With her radical spiked haircut and her hip New York clothes, Randy teaches everyone just how much fun it is to be different.

Allison Cloud is a Native American Indian. Allison's super-smart and really beautiful. But she has one major problem: She's thirteen years old, five foot seven, and still growing!

Here's what they're talking about in
Girl Talk

SABRINA: So Randy, how is practice going with your new band.

RANDY: It's okay. But the lead singer, Troy is giving me a major hard time.

SABRINA: Why? He's so cool. And besides, he's gorgeous.

RANDY: He is kind of cute, but I don't think he's exactly thrilled about having a girl in the band.

SABRINA: Don't worry, Randy. I'm sure he knows you're the best drummer around. And I've seen the way he acts around you.

RANDY: What do you mean?

SABRINA: I think he thinks you're cute!

DRUMMER GIRL

By L. E. Blair

GIRL TALK® series created by Western Publishing Company, Inc.

Produced by Angel Entertainment, Inc.

Western Publishing Company, Inc., Racine, Wisconsin 53404

ISBN: :0-307-22010-9   A B C D E F G H I J K L M

Text by Naomi Wolfensohn

Chapter One

"Signorina Zak, stop banging those pencils on your desk!" Signora Capelli yelled from the front of the classroom. *"Prego!"*

Startled, I looked up. I really didn't think I was making that much noise. Sometimes I think she can hear a pin drop in the next state.

"How many times do I have to tell you not to do that in my class," Signora Capelli said in an icy tone, glaring at me over the tops of her glasses.

I got the point. Besides, I was not "banging" on my desk — I was drumming. There happens to be a major difference. One is noise and the other music. I wouldn't have been using pencils to begin with, but Signora Capelli had banned my drumsticks from the classroom at the beginning of the semester.

Since she is the teacher and all that, I stopped. In fact, I tried really hard to pay total attention until class was over. It wasn't easy either — conjugation of future tenses in Italian is a difficult thing to focus on first thing Monday morning.

I had signed up for Italian in the first place because I thought it would be fun. I used to go to Italian movies with my dad before my parents got divorced. He's a video and music director and he's totally into foreign films.

I also love Italian food — spaghetti, tortellini, lasagna, fettucini, calzone, ravioli, pizza. I was convinced that Italian was going to be a fun class but so far, fun is not one of the adjectives I would use to to describe Signora Capelli.

Finally, the period was over. I grabbed my drumsticks from the back pocket of my black jeans and headed out into the hall. Even though I think Acorn Falls, Minnesota, is a small town — especially compared to my home town, New York City — the halls at Bradley Junior High get pretty crowded between classes.

"Randy!" someone called out from behind me. "Randy, wait up!"

I turned and saw one of my best friends, Sabrina Wells, fighting her way toward me.

"*Bonjourno*, Sabs," I said when she finally reached me.

"Bon-whatever, Ran," Sabs began breathlessly, "I don't have much time. But tickets go on sale at lunch today and I want to make sure that everyone's going since we might not get to lunch at the same time and whoever does should get in line right away so we can get really good seats and . . ."

Sabs is incredible. She said all that without taking a single breath. "Breathe, Sabs," I interrupted, laughing. "What in the world are you talking about?"

Sabs took a deep breath, her hazel eyes wide with astonishment. "Randy Zak, don't you ever listen to morning announcements?" she asked, shaking her head.

She had me there. I usually don't listen to Mr. Hansen, the principal, when he talks to us over the loudspeaker. He usually announces teacher's meetings, sports practices, and stuff. I don't belong to a club or any kind of group, and I'm really not the student council type.

"Sabs, you know I don't," I said to her impatiently. "Listen, I've got to run or I'll be late for class." I turned and started walking down the hall again. All the teachers at Bradley are really particular about rules. And there are some major rules at Bradley. It's unreal. Bradley is nothing like my old school in New York City, which was sort of unstructured.

After my mom and I moved to Acorn Falls at the beginning of the year, I had a hard time adjusting to all the rules.

"Okay, okay," Sabs replied, walking really fast and trying to keep up with me. I have to admit, it's not easy — I do walk fast. "I'm talking about the Battle of the Bands. Tickets go on sale today."

"The Battle of the Bands?" I asked, stopping short. Sabs bumped into me.

"Right," Sabs said quickly. "You know, Acorn Falls has one every year. Mostly high school kids compete. It's really fun. Didn't you hear *any* of the announcements?"

I shook my head as the warning bell sounded. We had two minutes to get to class.

"Oh my gosh!" Sabs exclaimed. "I'm going to be late for band!"

"Then you'd better motor," I replied, turning up the stairs. "I'll see you in homeroom. *Ciao*."

"See ya!" Sabs called as she ran down the stairs toward the band room in the basement.

Hmm, a battle of the bands, I thought with interest as I slid into my math class a nanosecond before the final bell rang. Miss Munson raised her eyebrows at me, but didn't say anything.

As we started doing percentages, I wondered if this Battle of the Bands would be any good. We never had one in New York, but that might be because my school was kind of small. Anyway it sounded like a more suburban kind of thing to do. I definitely wanted to know more about this competition, but I would have to wait until homeroom next period. Math droned on endlessly, as always.

I think that a great horror movie could be called, *The Never-Ending Math Period*. In the movie, the clock would get stuck on the minute right before the bell is supposed to ring. And the hand would jump at the end of the minute so everyone would think it was going to move. But it never would. It would always be a minute before class ends. Kids would like go crazy and turn into cannibals or something.

This is the kind of stuff that I think of right

before I fall asleep at night. I love horror movies. I think I want to write horror movies when I grow up.

Luckily, the clock in our classroom worked. The bell rang and math was finally over. Even though I was supposed to meet Sabs in homeroom and hear more about the Battle of the Bands, I took my time. I knew that Sabs would run into a million people and have a million conversations before she got to homeroom.

My two other best friends, Katie Campbell and Allison Cloud, are also in my homeroom, and I spotted them when I walked in. They had their heads together and were busy talking about an English paper when I slid into the desk behind them. The two of them talk about school a lot, even when they're not in school. Secretly I think It's a little unnatural, but they seem to enjoy it.

"Hi, Randy," Allison said, turning around to look at me. Al is really great. She is one hundred percent Chippewa. I think that's really cool. I'd never known a Native American before I met Al. Hard to believe after having lived in New York City, where there are so many kinds of people, but it's true.

6

"*Bonjourno*!" I greeted them. "What's up, kids?"

"Randy, Sabs said you didn't even know about the Battle of the Bands," Katie answered, incredulous. "They've had thousands of announcements. How could you not have heard about it?"

I shrugged. "Don't know," I replied briefly and took out my drumsticks. I beat a tempo on the notebook in front of me. "I wasn't listening."

"So, are you going?" Katie asked me.

"Yeah, I guess so. Why not, it sounds interesting," I replied.

Then Katie turned to Allison. "You're going, aren't you Al?"

"I hadn't really thought about it," Al replied softly.

"Well, you can't sit at home if we're all there," I said firmly. Sometimes I don't think Al would do anything if we weren't around to make sure she did. She would be just as happy staying home for hours and reading a book, as she would be to go out. It's a wonder we're friends. I get crazed if I have to hang out in one place too long.

"That's true, Allison," Katie put in. "So I guess it's settled, then. We're all going."

"All going where?" Sabs suddenly asked, throwing herself into the chair next to mine. She paused for a moment, trying to catch her breath. I was sure she had run all the way to class from her locker. "All going where?" she repeated, pulling her long red curly hair back into a ponytail. Sabs has really great hair that she's constantly complaining about even though we all think it's gorgeous. "I can't believe I forgot my English book again. This has got to stop."

I laughed. Sabrina is always saying that things have to stop. She is really into self-improvement. At the beginning of the year, she actually carried around a pink spiral notebook that she called her self-improvement notebook. She wrote all kinds of stuff in it about trying to be punctual and maintaining her composure. She says it's helped her a lot, but personally, I think Sabs is really cool the way she is.

"We're all going to the Battle of the Bands," Katie replied to Sabs' question. That's one thing about Katie, she doesn't get sidetracked easily. She has lots of determination and gets things done. She's into action, like I am. Like earlier this year she joined the boys' ice hockey team — and now she's one of their best players. I admire that.

"It's going to be awesome!" Sabs exclaimed. "The bands were great last year! Hey, is Spike's band going to be in it?"

I laughed again. "Sabs, if I knew whether or not Spike's band, Wide Awake was going to be in the Battle of the Bands, then I'd know about the Battle of the Bands in the first place, right?"

"Oh, yeah," Sabs replied, pulling a pen out of her purse. "That makes sense. Well, could you find out?"

Sabs kind of has a crush on Spike. Spike was one of the first people I met when I moved here, but he's in ninth grade. Katie, Sabs, Al and I are in the seventh grade so we go to a different school. I see Spike all the time though because he lives down the road from me and my mom is good friends with his mom.

Anyway, Spike's band is really good. They have a Stevie Ray Vaughn/Eric Clapton kind of sound that surprised me. That sounds kind of snobby, I know. But I mean, Acorn Falls, Minnesota, is not the music haven that New

York City is, by any stretch of the imagination.

Thinking about it, though, I was pretty positive that Wide Awake wouldn't be in the Battle of the Bands. They're more into jamming and just making music. Spike is always saying that as long as he can play, he doesn't care where.

I was just about to tell Sabs all of this when Ms. Staats walked into the classroom. For a teacher, she's actually kind of cool. Not that she lets us get away with anything, but you can tell that she tries to understand us.

While Ms. Staats took attendance and Mr. Hansen made the usual announcements, I wondered how this Battle of the Bands was going to be. As far as I knew, there was only one decent band in Acorn Falls besides Wide Awake — and that was a group called Iron Wombat. They have kind of an Elvis Costello sound. They play their own music, which is a refreshing change from all the Bon Jovi cover groups around here. Iron Wombat's music is pretty good, but their lyrics aren't exactly great — in fact, they're pretty bad. The more I thought about it, the more I realized I had to find out about this competition thing.

Chapter Two

"Oh, Randy!" my mom called out to me as I was about to walk out the door. It was almost seven o'clock and I was on my way to the supermarket. I wanted to make sure I got there before it closed.

I paused in the open doorway, looking back at her. "What, M?" My friends think it's really weird that I call my mother M and my father D. Even though I admit it sounds strange in Minnesota, it didn't sound all that bizarre in New York City. After all, Sheck, who's my best friend in New York, calls his parents by their first names, too.

"I need more newspapers," M replied, a little distracted.

"No prob, M," I said. "More newspapers."

M's kind of young still, only thirty-two. She dropped out of art school to marry D. She was basically just Mrs. Zak for twelve years, going to all these parties and openings and stuff every night. My father directs commercials and music videos so they went out a lot when we lived in New York. After the divorce and moving here, M finally got back into her art.

Lately, M's been in this papier-mache stage. She says she has to explore all her artistic impulses because she's been away from it for so long. Her painting stage is over for the moment. Now there are wild sculptures lying all over our barn. Yup, our barn. See, we live in this converted barn. After growing up in apartments my whole life, I had to make quite an adjustment. But I love it. The whole downstairs is one huge room, except the bathroom. My mother put up wooden screens in one corner to make space for her bedroom area. The kitchen is off in another corner, the living room is in the front of the room and M has a studio in the back. My room is upstairs in what used to be the hayloft. It's kind of small up there, but since there's enough room for my drums, I'm happy.

"'Bye, M," I said and walked through the door.

"See ya, hon," I heard M call as I shut the door behind me.

12

I shook my head as I dropped my skateboard onto the driveway. M is nothing like any of my friends' mothers. Sometimes she gets so into "creating" that she forgets to do things. You know basic things, like eating and sleeping.

When I got to the grocery store, I flipped up my skateboard, grabbed it and headed inside. I like to do the food shopping. M gives me a list but I can always improvise if I feel like it. I love to improvise.

Not that I can go crazy. For instance, M doesn't allow sugar in the house unless it's in ice cream. I'm not a big junk food addict anyway, but what's the harm in a Twinkie once in a while? But I can just hear her, "Do you know what they put in those things? The preservatives? Don't eat it, Ran." She likes to say that we shouldn't eat food that could exist for longer than we can.

Anyway, the grocery store wasn't too crowded. Not that I really mind when it is. I like to read the *National Enquirer* while I wait on line. You know, stories like, "*Woman Gives Birth to Two-headed Baby* and *Who Is Elvis's Kid*?" How anybody can take that stuff seriously is beyond me.

"Randy!" I heard somebody call from the produce aisle.

I pushed my cart over and saw Sabs standing by the kiwi fruit.

"What's up, Sabs?" I asked, stopping in front of her. "What's with all that kiwi?"

Sabs had about ten kiwis in her nearly full cart and two more in her hand.

"It's a new diet I read about in *Young Chic Magazine*," Sabs explained. Sabs has more magazine subscriptions than a dentist's office. She's always reading diets and goes on a new one every other week.

"Another one?" I asked sighing. "What's this one called?"

"It's the Ten-day Kiwi/Mango diet," Sabs replied. "What's a mango look like anyway?"

I laughed.

"Giggling in the produce section," Mr. Wells suddenly remarked as he walked up behind us. "Isn't that illegal in fourteen states?"

"Dad!" Sabs exclaimed.

I think it's cool that Mr. Wells does the food shopping. I don't think my father was ever in a grocery store. Come to think of it, I don't think my mother was either. In New York City, you just call up a grocery store and they can deliver all that stuff. Anyway, the Wells have a division of labor in their house. There are four kids living at home, (Sab's oldest brother is away at college) so Mr. Wells does the grocery shopping with a different kid every week. You can always tell who went with Mr. Wells by the food in the house. Obviously, this was Sabs' week.

"How ya' doing, Randy?" Mr. Wells asked, turning to me. "You're not going on this nuts, berries, hay, straw, and twig diet, too, are you?"

"Dad!" Sabs exclaimed again.

Mr. Wells really loves to tease Sabs. It's probably because she's his only daughter out of five kids. Sabs is easy to tease, but she takes it well. I think it's a great combination to find in a person.

"All right, all right," he conceded. "Listen, I'll be on line at the deli. Meet me there. Okay?"

"Well, I've got to get moving ," I said after he had walked away. "We haven't eaten yet."

"Oh, no!" Sabs said, sounding horrified.

"What? What's the matter, Sabs?" I asked startled.

"You haven't eaten?" She said loudly.

"No," I replied patiently. I had just said that I hadn't eaten. Obviously, Sabs was trying to make a dramatic point. I looked at her without saying a word.

Finally, after a few seconds of watching Sabs squirm while she waited for me to ask her why, I needed to eat, I gave in. "Why ,should I have eaten, Sabs?" I asked, grinning at her.

"Randy, you should never go food shopping on an empty stomach," she replied solemnly.

I must have shown my disbelief because Sabs continued quickly. "Randy, it's a fact. Think about it. You're hungry, so you're going to buy a lot of stuff — a lot more food than you would normally eat. And because you haven't eaten, you want to eat now. So you're going to buy something that you can eat right way. Probably junk food. Am I right?"

I laughed. "You're right," I added. I didn't want her to think I was making fun of her. Even Sabs has her limits. "So I better jam before I get even hungrier."

Sabs agreed and then said that she had to go find someone to tell her what a mango looked like anyway.

I put on my headphones and turned up the volume on my Walkman. My Walkman is like an extension of my body. I am practically never without it — I can't imagine life without music. The sounds of Buddy Rich filled my ears. Buddy Rich was an amazing drummer. It's so wild to have an album full of just drumming.

Zipping up and down the aisles, I thought about what to make for dinner. M had left that up to me. As I reached for a frozen pizza, I realized that Sabs was right. I was too hungry to be shopping. M would never eat pizza. I decided we needed a quick chicken stir fry instead, so I headed back to the produce aisle.

After I finished, I picked up a stack of newspapers and headed for the express lane. If I can help it, I never get more than two bags of groceries. I planned to get only one bag tonight go I could ride my skateboard and carry the newspapers and stuff. Skateboarding and carrying groceries at the same time is not exactly easy. It snows so much in Acorn Falls that I use every clear day possible to skateboard. Sabs and her father had just come through the check-out line as I finished paying for my groceries.

"Can we give you a ride home, Randy?" Mr.

Wells asked as he and Sabs pushed their cart over to my lane.

"No, thanks," I replied, picking up my skateboard and the two bags of groceries.

Besides, even though it was dark outside, it felt totally different from nighttime in New York City. I always feel safe here in Acorn Falls. It's like the town is out of a time warp or something. Everyone is so nice. But I have to admit that sometimes I actually miss the impersonal rudeness of New York.

The three of us walked out of the store together.

"Hey, Randy, look at this!" Sabs suddenly exclaimed. We were standing in that no-man's land between the two automatic doors. She was staring at one of those big bulletin boards where people hang up lost cat notices and car-for-sale signs.

"What?" I asked, pausing on the mat, keeping the outside door open.

Sabs pointed to a white sign. The bottom of the sign was torn into little strips that each had a phone number on them. A lot of the tags for the sign had already been pulled off.

I peered at it.

DRUMMER WANTED
Band searching for someone to keep the beat.
Experience necessary.
If interested call the number below:

"Talk about vague," I replied. "They don't even say what kind of music they play. Hey listen Sabs, I better motor home. M must be starving by now."

"Randy, didn't you look at the name on those tags?" Sabs asked incredulously, grabbing my arm.

I was about to answer her, when I suddenly realized that I was curious. I mean, music is my thing.

"Troy Tanner," I read off the bottom of the sign. "Yeah, so?"

"Randy!" Sabs replied, exasperated.

"Sabrina, if you let me by, I'll bring the car around," Mr. Wells suddenly cut in. "Then you and Randy can finish your conversation in private. Okay?"

"Sorry, Dad," Sabs said, giggling. "I forgot you were there."

"Obviously," he said with a grin. He

squeezed by their cart, which was totally full of bags and headed out toward the parking lot.

"Randy!" Sabs said again. "Troy Tanner!"

"So?" I repeated, getting a little impatient. The name meant nothing to me.

"Troy Tanner is the lead guitarist and singer for Iron Wombat," Sabs finished, looking at me triumphantly.

"Oh," I replied. "I guess they won't be competing in the Battle of the Bands, then." I paused for a moment. "Well, unless they get someone right now. It's three weeks away, right?"

"Right," Sabs replied. "So, you should probably call right away." She reached over and ripped off a tag and handed it to me.

"Oh, no!" I exclaimed, "I'm not joining Iron Wombat. No way, no how."

Sabs should never play poker. She has one of those faces that shows everything she's feeling. At that moment she looked completely disappointed.

"Why not?" she asked, wrinkling her forehead in confusion. "You said yourself that they're one of the few bands around here with talent. Why wouldn't you want to be their drummer?"

"I don't join things," I answered immediately. "I just don't." Just then I heard Mr. Wells start the station wagon. Their car's got this little backfiring problem. You can hear it a mile away.

"What kind of reason is that?" Sabs wanted to know. "What do you mean, you don't join things?"

"Just that," I said shortly. "I'm not into the group thing — you know, clubs and sports teams and stuff. It's not me, okay?"

"Okay, Randy," Sabs finally replied, as her father pulled up to the curb. "But promise me you'll think about it."

"All right," I conceded, shoving Troy's number into the pocket of my jeans. "I'll think about it."

"Thanks," Sabs said, rolling her cart up to the back of their station wagon where all this black smoke was coming out of the tailpipe. "Sure you don't want a ride?"

I looked at the cloud of exhaust and raised my eyebrow at Sabs. "I think I'll skateboard."

Sabs giggled. "Okay, I'll see you tomorrow then."

"*Ciao*," I called out and then jumped on my board.

Skateboarding home, I did think about it. Iron Wombat had some serious kicking tunes, but their lyrics were about as exciting as a wet dishrag. Nope, I had decided that I meant what I said to Sabs. I'm definitely not a joiner. Buddy Rich hadn't needed to be part of a band. And neither did I.

Chapter Three

"Good, you're back," M said as soon as I walked into our barn. "Sheck called."

"He did?" I asked, a little surprised. I had talked to him only the week before. I didn't expect to hear from him so soon. "Can I call him back now?"

"Sure, but don't stay on too long," M replied, turning back to her sculpture. "Did you get some newspapers?"

"Yup." I walked over and dropped the stack at the base of her stool. I never realized how heavy newspapers were. I could never be a paper person and deliver them every day — especially on a skateboard.

"Thanks," M said distractedly as she reached for the one on the top of the stack.

I carried the rest of the groceries over to the kitchen counter. Picking up the phone, I put the wok on the stove.

"Hey, Adian," I said as Sheck's father answered the phone. "Sheck around?"

"If it isn't Randy Zak!" Adian exclaimed. "How ya' doing, kid? We miss you around here. Sheck hasn't been the same since you've gone away. He's lost the will to live. He doesn't eat, doesn't sleep. In fact, he doesn't leave the apartment at all. So how's life in the slow lane?"

I laughed. Adian can be kind of weird sometimes, but he is pretty cool. He's a writer — mostly New Age Science Fiction stuff. I tried reading one of his books once, but it's like reading something from another stratosphere.

"I'm sure Sheck's here, since he never leaves," Adian continued. "But I'm not sure if he's up to talking. Did I mention the vow of silence he's taken?"

I laughed again. Sheck is worse than most girls I know. He practically never shuts up. He would probably explode if he ever took a vow of silence.

"Ran!" Sheck exclaimed, coming to the phone. "Where were you before?"

"I was at the grocery store," I said, opening a package of chicken.

"Oh," he replied, quietly. I grabbed the cutting board and put it over the sink. Then I started cleaning the chicken.

"So what's going on, Sheck?" I asked, figuring something must have come up for him to call me again so soon. "What did you call for?"

"I just felt like it," Sheck answered defensively. "Is that a crime?"

Hey! What's with him I thought to myself. *Afterall he called me. What's he so upset about.* "Hit rewind Sheck. Let's replay this, okay?"

Sheck didn't answer.

"Sheck *darling*, I'm so so glad you called," I said, imitating one of those women from late-night movies on TV. "Y'know, I practically miss you to death. Just hearing your voice . . .well, it makes my entire week. In fact, you don't even have to say anything. Just knowing you're on the other end, breathing, is enough for me. Breathe for me, *darling* please."

Sheck cracked up. I knew that would get him.

"You are a really warped child," he said after he had stopped laughing. "Do you know that?"

"Well, you taught me everything I know,

Sheckster," I replied as I started to chop vegetables for the stir fry.

"And you were such an apt pupil," he shot back. "Listen, Randy, I'm sorry about a moment ago. I'm still not used to you living in another state and I . . . ."

"Forget it," I cut him off. One thing I really think is unnecessary are apologies, especially where Sheck is concerned. "So what's up with you?" I asked as I put a pot of water for rice on the back burner.

"Nothing earth-shaking," he said. "I mean, I just felt like talking to you. What's new? Olivia said she was into a paper stage."

M won't let my friends call her Mrs. Zak. Sometimes, Allison and Katie have a major problem calling her Olivia. I think Sabs gets a kick out of it, though.

"Sheck, you should see this place!" I explained, lighting the stove and pouring oil into the wok. "There are papier mache creatures everywhere. I hope she doesn't get into metal stuff after this. I don't quite know if I trust her with a blow torch."

"Can you imagine Olivia with a blow torch?" Sheck asked, laughing. "Scar-ry! Hey, that might make a great slice-and-dice type flick, don't you think? Mad artist cuts loose with blow torch! That would be totally fab!"

Sheck shares my warped love of hack-and-splatter movies. We used to have horror movie marathons all the time. "Really," I agreed. "Think of the graphic gore scenes that we could get from a blow torch."

Last year, in New York, Sheck and I did a critique of a bunch of horror flicks for school. It was kind of wild to sit around watching Blood Diner and The Newlydeads and call it homework.

"So what's new with Sabrina, Allison and Katie?" Sheck asked, changing the subject.

I dropped the chicken in the wok and started stirring. The trick to a successful stir fry is to start with the food that takes the longest to cook and then add soft things like tomatoes last. "Not much," I replied, as I added a little soy sauce to the chicken. Soy sauce is important in a stir fry, too.

"Tell them I said, hey," Sheck continued. Sheck had come to visit over Thanksgiving weekend. My friends loved him. Even Stacy Hansen, the class snob and someone who is definitely not my friend, thought he was "a major hunk." Hunk must be a small-town kind of word. I always want to ask, "Hunk of what?" I'm proud to say that I've never used that word before in my life — except when referring to cheese or bread.

"Will do," I replied, dumping bamboo shoots into the wok. Bamboo shoots are kind of hard and take a while to soften up. "In fact, I just saw Sabs at the grocery store tonight. She was trying to get me to try out for this band — the Iron Wombats — they needs a drummer. And it's not like they're a new band or anything. They're actually pretty good. They have a kind of an Elvis Costello sound. They even write their own stuff. And their music pumps — not that I can say the same about their lyrics. Sabs just doesn't understand that I'm not into joining something like that. I want to be a solo drummer. I don't want to get into the band scene."

Sheck didn't answer.

"Well, Sheck?" I asked, banging my wooden spoon against the side of the wok for emphasis. "This is the part where you're supposed to say something about how much you agree and that group stuff is not for me."

I paused, but Sheck didn't jump in. In fact, I could barely hear him breathing.

"Sheck?" I asked warningly. "I'm not interested in being in a little Battle of the Bands thing, okay?"

That got him. "A Battle of the Bands?" he echoed, sounding interested. "Really?"

"Now, don't you start!" I exclaimed. "I'm tired and too hungry to talk about this."

"Okay, okay," Sheck replied. "But R.Z., (Sometimes Sheck just calls me by my initials), about this Battle of the Bands thing, what's the prize?"

I sighed. "I don't know. Does it matter?" I asked, dumping a cup of dry rice into the boiling water on the back of the stove and then scooping the rest of the vegetables into the wok.

"Of course it does," Sheck replied. "Check it out, okay?"

I didn't answer.

"R.Z.?" he asked and then continued without waiting for an answer. "Listen, girl, even Buddy Rich had to start somewhere. I think you should give it a chance. It might not be so bad being in a band. Give it some thought. Put the gray matter on the case, okay?"

He paused, and I still didn't say anything.

"Okay?" Sheck asked again, but this time much more firmly.

"Okay, okay," I replied. "Listen, Sheckster, I think my stir fry is just about done. And I've got to chow now or I will expire immediately."

"Got it," Sheck said. "It was good talking to you, Randy. You take care of yourself, all right?"

"Don't I always?" I asked, turning off the stove.

"Yeah," Sheck answered. "Listen, when is this Battle of the Bands anyway?"

"I don't know," I replied, suddenly suspicious. I don't know why, but I've known Sheck for a long time and he had a certain tone in his voice that sounded all too familiar . . . "Why?"

"I just wondered," he said.

"Three weeks, I think," I said. "Dinner's ready, so I've got to go."

"Okay, R.Z.," Sheck replied. "I'll speak on you soon, all right?"

"Got it," I said. "Say hey to everybody for me . . . . And thanks for calling. It really was good to hear you breathe."

Sheck laughed. "See ya!"

"Ciao!" I said and hung up the phone. "M!" I called. "Soup's on!"

As M cleaned up and I set the table, I thought about what Sheck had said. . I mean, I didn't exactly agree with him, but maybe he had a point. I did have to start somewhere. And Iron Wombat is a pretty decent band. That phone number was still in my pocket. I just might make another phone call after dinner.

Chapter Four

The next day after school I went to Troy Tanner's house. I'd called the night before to set up a time for an audition and here I was, drumsticks in hand. M had driven me over with my drums and I was ready. I knocked.

After a minute the door opened. "Can I help you?" a guy who I figured must be Troy Tanner asked. He looked at me as if he had no clue at all who I was, which kind of bugged me since I'd set this whole thing up with him the night before. He had dirty blond hair cut in a style Sheck and I call "nouveau preppie." You know, with the hair cut short in the back, but long in the front and parted all the way over on one side. This guy's hair was totally falling into his right eye.

"I'm Randy Zak," I announced loudly.

The guy just stared at me, his brown eyes blank, and he didn't say anything. I tapped my

32

foot in frustration, trying not to get mad. But really, we'd already talked about this. What was his problem?

"Are you Troy Tanner? I called last night about drumming in Iron Wombat," I continued, holding up my drumsticks. Did this guy need everything spelled out, or what?

"You're Randy Zak?" the guy finally replied, looking me up and down.

I was wearing exactly what I had worn to school — big black turtleneck, cut-off, rolled up jean shorts, black cable-knit tights, granny boots and of course, my black leather bomber jacket. So, what was he looking at?

"Last time I checked," I replied, confused. Was he going to keep me standing on the porch all day?

"But you're a girl," the guy said in surprise.

This guy was getting on my nerves. "You are Captain Obvious, aren't you?" I shot back. I rolled my eyes. "Look," I said slowly, "My name is Randy Zak and I came here to try out for your band. Do you want me to play outside, or what? It'll only take me a minute to set up on your porch." I gestured to the pile of drums behind me. Sometimes I really wish I played something light and transportable like the flute. Drums are not exactly easy to travel with.

The guy stepped back and flipped his hair, as if he was going to let me into the house. But then he stopped short and his eyes narrowed. "How old are you, kid?" he suddenly asked. "You look young."

Kid? He couldn't be more than fourteen himself. "Are you Troy?" I asked.

"Yeah," Troy replied.

"Well, do you need a drummer, or what?"

"Is that the guy who called you last night? The drummer?" somebody suddenly asked. A black kid with a high top fade had come up behind Troy. He stepped onto the porch and stood beside Troy. He stopped short as soon as he caught sight of me, his brown eyes widening in surprise. "It's a girl!" he announced.

I shook my head. These guys were unreal. What was this, the Dark Ages? Girls could play rock 'n' roll too.

The two of them were staring at me as if I were some kind of alien. I was sure that Buddy Rich had never gone through anything like this.

"Look, you guys obviously have problems

dealing with the idea of a girl drummer. Why don't you give me a call after you've figured out who Sheila E. is?" I said angrily. I turned quickly and walked down the porch steps. I paused when I saw my set of drums and debated my next move. How was I going to cart this stuff home by myself?

"Hey, wait a minute," the black kid called and jumped off the porch. He caught up to me and grabbed my arm. "We just weren't expecting a girl. Troy said you were a guy."

I didn't say a thing. So I happen to have a deep voice — big deal.

"Listen, I'm Alton," he continued, holding out his hand.

I stared at his hand for a moment, then decided to try one more time. Besides, I didn't want to tell Sheck I had chickened out. I took Alton's hand and shook it. "Randy Zak," I replied with my best smile.

Alton grinned. "I play bass," he said and then looked at my pile of drums. "Need help with these?"

"Sure," I answered and then bent down to pick up my cymbal stand. "Where do you want me to set up?"

"We practice in the garage," Alton said, grabbing my snare drum and my stool. "It's around back."

"Not so fast," Troy suddenly cut in, walking down the porch steps. "I don't know about this. Dude, it's bad enough she's a girl. But she's just a kid. We can't let her join Iron Wombat." Then he turned to me and flipped his hair again. "Don't waste your time — or ours — kid. You need a ride home?"

I opened my mouth to say something, but Alton beat me to it.

"Cool your jets, Troy," he said, balancing my drum on his hip. "We've had six dudes answer the ad and you know they all sound like a drum-by-numbers recording, or like they learned through the mail or something. We've only got three weeks to find a drummer. Besides, she's here so why not just let her do her thing?"

"Alton . . ." Troy began warningly, but I wouldn't let him finish. Enough was enough.

"Don't do me any favors, okay?" I interrupted. "I'm going home like I said before."

"Troy, you know Jim is as fed up as I am," Alton said, ignoring me. He walked toward the back of the house. "Give her a chance."

I just stood there for a minute, trying to decide what to do. Alton seemed okay but this Troy character was way out of line.

But I figured that since I was here I might as well go for it. So I grabbed the bass drum case and followed Alton. So maybe Troy was a jerk, but that didn't mean Iron Wombat's music wasn't good. Anyway, Troy's attitude only made me determined to show him that I wasn't just some kid, but that I could really play the drums. The garage door was open and I could see a third guy with a crew cut inside. He was wearing earphones and playing scales on a keyboard. I figured that he must be Jim.

Alton set up my drum and stool in the back of the garage while I opened my bass drum case. Troy showed up in the doorway, empty-handed.

"Fine, you can try out, kid. But you've got to cart your own equipment," he said grudgingly.

This guy was cruising for a bruising. "You're quite a guy," I muttered loud enough for Troy to hear. Then I went and collected the rest of my stuff.

A few minutes later, I was all set up. Jim had taken off his earphones and introduced himself. With a red crew cut and lots of freckles, Jim was not quite the image of rock and roll, but he sounded pretty good when he warmed up on the keyboards. So, what did it matter what he looked like?

I adjusted my stool, sat down and tested my drums. I sent my sticks flying over the drums, gave a little flourish and twirled my drumsticks when I had finished. Then I looked expectantly at Troy. "Ready, Killer?"

Alton shot me an admiring glance. "Hey! You can play, kid!" he exclaimed.

I sighed. "My name is Randy," I said slowly. "I don't answer to `kid.' And of course I can play — I told you I'm a drummer."

Troy snorted and strapped on his guitar. "Let's see what you're made of, Kid," he said, then paused. "Oh, sorry. I meant Randy." Biting back my tongue, I didn't reply.

"How about "Punch the Clock" by Elvis Costello?" Troy asked Alton and Jim. Then he looked back at me. "Do you know that?"

I nodded and got set. I was going to blow Troy Tanner out of the water with my drumming. Not only do I know the song "Punch the Clock" but I happen to like it. By the time I was finished, Mr. Troy Tanner would never know what had hit him.

Chapter Five

"Well?" Sabs asked impatiently the next day when I joined my best friends in the lunch-room. "What happened? How did it go?"

I had planned to call everybody the minute I got home, but I was starving so I ate something. Then I guess I didn't realize how exhausted I was because I fell asleep on the couch before I got a chance to call anyone.

"Yeah, Ran, how were the try-outs?" Allison asked excitedly. Are you in the band?

Sabrina cut in, "What's Troy really like?" Sabs opened her lunch bag and emptied six kiwis and a mango out onto the table.

"Everything's cool," I said, laughing. "I'm an Iron Wombat now."

"You made it!" Sabs squealed. "That's awesome!"

"That's great, Randy," Katie added, smiling

40

at me.

I nodded. "I guess it's okay. But Troy gave me a major hard time. He has this thing about girls playing rock and roll. And he kept calling me kid."

"He calls *you* kid?" Katie asked, perplexed. "How old is he?"

"Don't know," I replied, taking a bite of my pita and egg-salad sandwich. "Fourteen, fifteen tops."

"Fourteen," Sabs added. Sabs always amazes me. She's one of those people who know everything about everybody. And since she has four older brothers, she usually does get the scoop on everyone.

"He's only two years older than you and he calls you *kid*?" Katie asked. "Is he serious? What's wrong with him?"

"Well, Katie," Sabs began, pausing in the middle of peeling a kiwi, "he could be like an old fourteen. You know how some guys seem really old for their ages, some seem to act their age and others seem really young? Like Sam is definitely a young twelve. Well, maybe Troy is an old fourteen." She turned her attention back to her fruit.

There was a long pause. "Well, Sabrina has spoken," I commented and waved my hand ceremoniously.

Al, Katie and Sabs giggled.

"So tell us everything," Sabrina commanded. "What happened? And what do you mean that Troy gave you a hard time? Why?"

"I haven't got a clue," I replied. "It was wild. He just stared at me like I was from another planet when he answered the door. The bass player, Alton, finally came out and helped me carry my drums out back. And then we jammed."

"That's it?" Sabs prodded. "You know, Randy, when I say everything, I mean it. You are terrible at telling stories. What about details? What was Troy wearing? Is he really cute up close? I saw the band once, is Alton the black guy? What about the other guy? What's his name?"

Katie laughed. "That's a lot for Randy to notice, Sabs," she pointed out.

"After all," Al added diplomatically, "People see what they're interested in. So let's ask Randy about the music. Were they good?"

"We jammed," I replied. "And at first, we

played for almost forty-five minutes. After that they had a big fight about whether or not to let me in the group. Alton and Jim voted yes, but Troy has this hang-up about me being younger and being a girl."

"And then what?" Sabs asked impatiently.

"I guess that's when I told them they could find another drummer," I said calmly.

"You didn't!" Sabs exclaimed, her mouth dropping open in surprise.

"She wouldn't make it up, Sabs," Katie added, spooning up the last of her yogurt. "And obviously, she changed her mind about them finding another drummer because she said she's one of the Iron Wombats now."

"How'd they get you to change your mind?" Sabs asked. "That's not the easiest thing in the world to do," she teased.

"Jim and Alton talked me into it," I replied. That wasn't totally true. I guess I wanted to be talked into it in some way. And I have to admit that I kind of liked Alton and Jim.

"Where'd they get a name like Iron Wombat anyway?" Sabs asked, changing the subject. "What in the world is a wombat?"

"It's an animal from Australia," Al

answered. Last summer, Allison had actually read over one hundred books — just for the heck of it. Talk about being master of trivia — Al's it. Sabs is constantly telling Allison that she should be on Jeopardy. I'm not one for game shows, but Sabs is probably right. Al would make a ton of cash.

"It's a marsupial and it kind of looks like a small bear," Al continued.

"What's a marsupial?" Sabs asked.

"You know, like a kangaroo," Katie explained. "It has a pouch and everything. Right, Al?" Allison nodded.

"I still don't get it," Sabs said. "Why'd they name their band Iron Wombat?"

I laughed. "I don't know, Sabs," I replied. "But if I get the chance, I'll find out, okay?"

"So when do you have practices?" Katie asked.

"Practically every day," I answered with a sigh. "We've only got three weeks to that Battle of the Bands and we're going to need every second of it."

"But, I thought you said Iron Wombat was good," Katie said confused.

"They are," I replied. "But my style is different from what they're used to, so we all have to have time to adjust."

"Different?" Sabs asked blankly. "What do you mean different?"

"Well, their last drummer only kept a beat," I explained. "Not to put that down or anything, but that's not how I play."

"Well, how do you play if you don't keep the beat?" Sabs asked, reaching for her last kiwi. She grimaced and bit into it. "I'm getting really sick of kiwis, by the way."

We all laughed.

"There must be more to drumming than keeping the beat, right Randy?" Allison asked with a smile."

I feel as if I've known Allison forever. She always says just the right thing. And it's weird, but she knows so much about me — more than anyone except Sheck really. And I've known Sheck practically my whole life. I haven't even known Allison a year.

"That's right," I replied, grinning back. "Of course, drums are fine for keeping the beat, but sometimes a song can be done entirely on the drums. The drum is an instrument you know."

"So you play a little fancier than Iron

Wombat's last drummer?" Katie asked, peeling a banana.

"Right," I said. "Iron Wombat is good, but they play by the book. Cut and dried. Boom-Boom, that's it. I want to get everybody rocking, you know what I mean. If yesterday's practice was any indication, they're definitely not used to letting loose."

"If I know you, Iron Wombat's about to change," Sabs said laughing. She picked up her mango. "Anyone have any idea how to eat this thing?"

"I think you've got to peel it," Katie replied, looking at Allison.

"Actually," Al began, "you should probably cut it like a melon. Then you can scoop out the pulp with a spoon and eat it like you'd eat a cantaloupe."

"Al, you know everything," Sabs said admiringly. "It's really incredible."

Allison blushed. "Good luck with practice, Randy," she said, turning back to me. Allison doesn't really like talking about herself. But she's great with everyone else's problems. She's better than some of the shrinks I've seen back in New York, that's for sure. Al would make a great psychiatrist even if she's always saying she wants to be a writer.

"I hope you can convince those guys to give your ideas a chance," Allison finished.

I did too. Otherwise, I didn't think I could last very long as a member of Iron Wombat.

Chapter Six

That afternoon at practice I started drumming the way I had told my friends I would. Actually, practice was going better than I had expected, and I thought we sounded great.

"Hold up! Hold up!" Troy called out suddenly. He waited until we had all stopped and it was quiet. Then he flipped his hair and turned toward me. "What are you doing?" he demanded.

The problem I had mentioned to my friends at lunch had obviously hit with full force. I didn't answer Troy, but just stared at him as if I didn't know what he was talking about. I wanted to see how big a problem this was going to be.

"What do you mean?" Alton asked, adjusting his guitar strap. "She sounds great. David never went off on riffs like that."

Riffs are a special kind of music for soloist. So someone could do riffs on the drums or on the piano or even sing them. I call it spotlight music.

"Right," Troy said through clenched teeth. "So why is she?" He spun around and glared at me again. "What are you up to, Kid? This band is not a showcase for your supposed talent. This is my band."

"Randy," I corrected him but didn't say anything else. I could tell that Troy was getting pretty miffed watching me sit there and twirl my drumsticks without answering him.

"Troy, what do you mean, *your band*?" Alton asked. "From what I remember, this is *our* band. Right, Jim?" Jim just nodded. I've noticed that he's really not much for words.

"You know that's what I meant," Troy said after a pause, giving his hair another flip. "Anyway now we have this kid, sor-ry, Randy, trying to take over."

That definitely got to me. "Relax, Troy," I said, losing my patience a little. "I'm just improvising a little on the drums — you know, jazzing things up a bit?"

"What!?" Troy retorted, sounding astounded. Bluntness is one of my trademarks. I guess Troy was just beginning to realize that.

"Troy, I'm not trying to take over the band. But I don't think drums should only be in the background either," I continued, twirling my sticks. "If there's an opening, I like to jump right in. Alton and Jim think I sound pretty good, right guys?" I turned toward them and flashed my biggest smile yet.

"She does sound good," Alton repeated.

"But Iron Wombat is known for it's kicking guitars, not it's drums," Troy sputtered, obviously not ready to give up yet.

Neither was I. "Well, that's true, but as they say in show biz — always keep 'em guessing," I countered. "Besides, I'm part of it now."

"Not if I had my way, you wouldn't be," Troy replied, taking a step toward me.

"Hey, hey," Alton said as he moved to stand between us. "Randy's right, man. It's a different band now. And she does sound great."

I nodded my thanks at Alton and looked back at Troy. This guy had major ego problems. He thought the whole band should revolve around him. It was obvious that he couldn't handle the thought that I might actually steal a little of his thunder.

"I don't like the sound," Troy stubbornly repeated. "It's not Iron Wombat. It's not what we're known for. Our fans won't even know it's us."

"Sure they will," I said cheerfully. "You still have the same old lyrics. They'll know it's Iron Wombat after they hear a song or two — no matter what I do."

Troy's eyes narrowed and Alton took a step back. "What do you mean by that?" Troy said softly.

"Well, now that you're asking me," I said slowly, "Most of your music really pumps. But the lyrics could use some work."

"I wrote those lyrics!" Troy exclaimed, flipping his hair out of his eyes. I decided that his teeth must really hurt the way he was clenching them so hard.

"Well . . . " I began and trailed off. What else could I say? Troy's music was great, but the lyrics were hurting. But I was beginning to realize that maybe this was to much to throw on old Troy all at once.

"You know, kid," Troy began, squeezing the neck of his guitar, "it was a major mistake to let you join Iron Wombat. You don't have the right attitude for us"

"Oh, come on, Troy," I replied calmly. I have to admit that I was beginning to enjoy watching how upset Troy was becoming. "You're not afraid of a few changes for the good of the band are you? Afterall, two big heads are better than one."

"Now, what is that supposed to mean?" he asked, squeezing the neck of his guitar even harder so that his knuckles turned white. In a minute, the whole neck was going to snap right off.

"I just mean a little change never hurt anybody," I replied, sitting back on my stool. Troy stalked toward me, stopping only when he was practically right on top of my drum set. Unplugging his guitar, he took off the strap and set his instrument in the stand.

"She's right," Jim suddenly said.

Wow! Was I surprised. Like I said, Jim is not the conversational type. Troy looked as surprised as I felt. He flipped his hair out of his eyes and turned to look at Jim.

"She's right," Jim repeated. "Our lyrics are pretty weak."

"Do you think so too?" Troy asked Alton.

Alton stared directly at Troy. It suddenly occurred to me that Troy and Alton were probably best friends. "Yeah, I agree with them," he said, quietly. Then he started running his fingers up and down the neck of his guitar.

"Why didn't you dudes say something sooner?" Troy demanded.

"I figured we couldn't do any better, so why make an issue of it?" Alton replied, still fingering his guitar strings.

When Troy turned and looked at Jim, Jim nodded his head in agreement with Alton.

"Don't tell me that your immense talents include writing lyrics," Troy suddenly said, turning back to me.

"Well . . . " I began and then paused. I had had a class in songwriting back in New York City. I remember Sheck and I took it absolutely certain that it was going to be a major blowoff class. Songwriting seemed as if it was going to be so easy. We had definitely found out otherwise. I'm no John Lennon, but I was sure that I could do better than Troy.

"Great!" Alton said loudly. "Then you can do the lyrics and Troy will do the music."

Troy groaned and threw his hands up in the air. "I don't believe this!" he exclaimed. "This is crazy, dudes. You really want her to write our songs?"

"It wouldn't hurt," Jim said quietly. He played a few scales up and down his keyboard.

"Just give it a try," Alton persuaded, fiddling with the knobs on his amp. "We need something new for the Battle of the Bands anyway."

"Why?" Troy asked in a last-ditch attempt to ditch me. "Why can't we just use "Jump Up and Shout" or something?"

"Everyone knows it," Alton replied. "It's played, dude. We need a new tune."

Troy looked as if he was going to say something else, but instead he reached for his guitar. "Fine," he said through gritted teeth. "Just fine."

Two hours later, I started packing up my drums. It had been a killer practice — probably because Troy was kind of mad. He drove us through two straight sets without a break. It was especially hard for me since I wasn't all that familiar with Iron Wombat's songs yet. I hoped that we wouldn't have to go through this for the next three weeks. I would never last.

Jim and Alton had packed up quickly and left. Again I wished that drums could be carted around like a flute.

"Kid," Troy called out. I ignored him. How many times did I have to tell him that I didn't answer to that name? Maybe action would speak louder than words.

"Kid!" Troy repeated, a little more loudly.

I continued to pack up my stuff — silently.

"Oh," Troy finally said after a long pause. "Sor-ry. I meant Randy."

I looked up. That was more like it. Of course, I could do without his attitude too. But two could play at this game. "What's up, Troy?" I asked.

Troy frowned and flipped his hair back. "Listen, Randy, I'm just about done with some new music," Troy answered me after a long pause. "I'll give it to you when I'm finished and you can do your thing."

"Excellent, Troy," I replied, closing one of my drum cases. *Uh-Uh, what do I do now*? I thought to myself. Troy was going to give me a score sheet full of music. I don't play guitar or keyboards, so it wasn't going to be easy to write words to music I couldn't fully hear? But I couldn't tell Troy that and give him the satisfaction of thinking that I couldn't handle it all.

"And remember, we're on a deadline," he added snidely.

"I will if you will," I shot back. This guy really knew how to push my buttons. But I wasn't going to let him see that. No way, no how.

"Fine," Troy replied and walked toward his house leaving me alone in the garage. Great. Now I had to come up with lyrics fast — and they had to be kicking!

Chapter Seven

"Randy! RANDY!" M screamed from the bottom of the steps leading up to my loft. "Randy, phone!"

I wiped the sweat from my face with a towel. I hadn't even heard the phone ring. Not that it was any wonder — I had been practicing my drums.

Jumping up from my stool, I clattered down the stairs after M. My sleeveless black T-shirt was practically dripping with sweat and even my black biker shorts were damp. I had really been working.

Picking up the phone in the kitchen, "Yo," I said into the receiver. That's the way I usually answer the phone.

"Randy? It's Troy."

Of all the voices I might have expected, his was probably at the bottom of the list. Ever since I had joined the band, a week and a half ago, Troy had been barely civil to me — as if politeness was just too much effort for him.

"Yeah?" I replied quickly.

"I finished the music," Troy announced as if he was waiting for congratulations. I sure didn't feel like congratulating him. It had taken him more than a week to finish the music. Now I only had a few days to write the lyrics. Then we still had a week before the Battle of the Bands to learn the tune. I would have to come up with the words practically overnight.

"Wonderful," I replied dryly. I still didn't want Troy to know how worried I felt. I had to prove that I could write better lyrics.

"I didn't want you to waste any time so I'd thought I'd drop it off tonight," Troy continued, I gripped the phone, trying to keep my temper.

"Drop it off?" I repeated. "Where?"

"At your house," Troy replied with a small chuckle. "Hey, could I have possibly caught the super-cool Randy Zak off guard. I don't believe it."

Troy actually had a sense of humor. I never would have guessed it.

"Remember it well Troy, since it won't happen again," I said, grinning in spite of myself. This was a whole new Troy Tanner.

"Don't worry, I've got the whole conversation taped," Troy replied. "I'll listen to it again and again. So can I come by now to drop this off? Are you busy?"

"What else would I be doing but beating a tatoo on my drums?" I answered. "But I could take a moment out to answer the door. *Ciao*."

"Hey, wait — Where do you live?" Troy asked quickly, before I could hang up the phone.

"Oh, yeah," I said, "I suppose you do need to know that information."

Troy laughed an incredibly loud laugh. I realized that I'd never heard him laugh before. He had one of those loud, totally uninhibited laughs. You know, the kind where everyone in the movie theater — including the guy in the projection booth — would be able to hear him. But it was cool. I like laughs like that. It was good to know that Troy Tanner was not totally caught up in what people thought of him — except for the "nouveau preppie" haircut. That definitely said image conscious. This guy was a bundle of contradictions.

"I live on the corner of Maple and Ninth," I added. "It's the big brown barn."

"Barn?" Troy echoed confused.

"Right," I replied, happy to have caught him off balance. "*Ciao*." And then I hung up.

"Do you want Chinese take-out tonight, Ran?" M asked walking over to the sink with a bowl of papier mache paste. She started to dump it down the sink.

"What are you doing, M?" I asked, my mouth hanging open in disbelief. And I had wondered why the sink had gotten clogged twice last week.

"Getting rid of this," she answered immediately, stopping mid-pour.

Shaking my head, I grabbed the bowl out of my mother's hand. "M, that stuff is going to stop up the sink," I explained. "You should throw it in a plastic garbage bag."

"Uhh, right. Sorry Ran. Sometimes I get so caught up with my work, I just don't know think about the practical side." M said all of this and reached for a plastic garbage bag. "I'll have to remember this, plastic, plastic." she mumbled walking away. Then she stopped and turned around, "I'm getting ready to paint some of the masks," she said. "And, oh about that Chinese . . . "

"Got it," I replied, picking up Ho Chin's take-out menu from our stack of restaurant menus by the phone. Moo Shu Vegetables and Shrimp Fried Rice sounded great.

After I ordered, I headed back upstairs. Putting on my headphones, I switched on a Buddy Rich album. Then I sat down at my drums, picked up my sticks and tried to keep up with him. Secretly I understand M very well. Sometimes, I really get into my music and I forget everything, too.

Twenty minutes later, the tape stopped. I took off my headphones and heard the sound of someone clapping. I turned my head toward the door and there was Troy Tanner, sitting on the top step of my stairs, applauding.

"That was wild!" he said, standing up.

"How long have you been there?" I asked, grabbing a towel. I was suddenly very embarrassed about being all sweaty.

"About ten minutes," he replied, walking over to me. "Who were you listening to?"

"Buddy Rich. Wanna hear?" I asked, turning the tape over and handing him my

Walkman.

He put the headphones on and pushed play. A few moments later, he turned it off. "That guy is incredible. How come I've never heard of him? Who does he play for?"

"Well he played for himself. In the Fifties and Sixties mostly, unfortunately he's not alive anymore." I replied, standing up. "Besides, you're not a into drumming that's why you haven't heard of him."

"Randy!" M called from downstairs. "What's up with that Chinese food? Do I have to go get it now?"

"You've got fifteen more minutes, M!" I called back.

"Who in the world is that?" Troy asked, sounding a little confused. "She said her name was Olivia when she answered the door and she was covered with orange and purple paint."

"That's my mother," I said, brushing past Troy and heading down the stairs. "She doesn't care for titles, you know like Mrs. and Ms. and stuff, so she likes to be called by her first name. But I call her M."

"Oh," was all Troy could said as he picked

up his jacket and followed me down the stairs.

"Where's your father?"

"New York," I replied shortly. "My parents are divorced."

"Hey, did you order enough for Troy?" M asked as the two of us stepped into the kitchen. She turned to Troy. "Have you eaten yet?"

"I had some pizza over at Alton's," Troy answered.

"Well, I'm sure you can fit some more food in," M said as she walked over toward the bathroom. "I guess I'll take a quick shower and then go."

I nodded my agreement and started taking out the plates to set the table. "Are you staying?" I asked Troy, pausing in front of the cabinet.

"I don't want to impose . . . " Troy began.

Troy Tanner didn't want to impose? Unreal. Maybe he had an evil twin brother in another dimension and they had switched places or something. The guy standing in front of me was being much nicer than I'd thought Troy Tanner could ever be. "Are you serious? M would probably get offended if you weren't here when she came back. She hasn't shown you her sculpture yet, has she?"

"Sculpture?" Troy echoed. "No. She just got a sculpture?"

I laughed. "No, she just finished making a few," I said, pointing to M's studio area. "She's an artist. And she likes to show people her stuff. So you better not jam before the tour." I grabbed three plates and headed over to the table.

"She's an artist?" Troy asked, sounding kind of surprised.

Nodding, I tripped over the guitar case laying by the table. "Is this yours?"

"Yeah," Troy replied, picking it up and moving it out of the way, toward the couch. "Sorry about that."

"That looks like an acoustic guitar," I said, kind of confused. Acoustic guitar was just another name for a regular guitar. I didn't think Troy was the type to play any instrument that wasn't plugged in.

"It is," Troy said, opening the case and pulling out his guitar. He strummed the strings and sat down on the couch. "I like to write music on this guitar and then play it on the other one. Kind of weird, but it works the best for me."

"All right, I'm leaving," M announced as she suddenly emerged from her room.

Troy stared at the transformation. I don't blame him. M is like a different person when she isn't wearing her work clothes. And in her black lycra leggings, cropped black sweater and black lace-up boots, she could almost pass for my sister. In fact, people have mistaken us for sisters. Most people would probably be flattered by that, I guess. But not M. She always says that means that people aren't taking her seriously enough.

"See you in a few," M continued as she grabbed her purse and headed out.

Troy looked at me as the door shut behind my mother. "You mother is really . . . different," he said slowly.

"Different from what?" I asked, knowing what he meant but acting as if I didn't.

"She's definitely not like my mom," Troy admitted, flipping his hair. "My mother is like Mrs. PTA or something. I can't imagine her ever getting take-out, either. She freaks when I order pizza."

"Well, I grew up in New York and I guess

it's different from Acorn Falls," I replied, going over to sit in the chair across from Troy.

"Well, do you want to hear the new tune?" Troy asked.

This was great. I had been worried that since I don't play guitar I might have to write the words to a tune I had never heard. And here Troy was offering to play it for me.

"I wasn't sure if you played guitar or even keyboard, so I decided to come prepared to play the music for you," Troy continued, not looking at me.

This was funny. Troy must have known all along that I wouldn't be able to write the lyrics without his help, and he wasn't giving me a hard time about it? He was being so thoughtful and nice. It was hard to believe that he was the same obnoxious guy I'd been fighting with for the past week and a half. Amazing!

"Great," I replied, trying to keep the total surprise I was feeling off my face.

I settled back in my chair and watched Troy as he adjusted the tension on the strings of his guitar. His hair flopped down over his eyes, but he didn't brush it back. It gave me an opportunity to study him without fear of being caught in the act, so to speak. Except for the haircut, there was something about Troy that reminded me of Spike.

They didn't necessarily look alike, but there was something about them — maybe because they were both talented musicians.

I looked at what Troy was wearing. He had on beat-up jeans and an old Replacements T-shirt and black high-top sneakers. It was a lot like something Spike would wear — except he'd probably have a Jim Croce T-shirt on or something. And they both have earrings.

But the similarity was more than just a surface thing. Whatever they had in common definitely had to do with their music. I knew Spike could get into playing and totally forget where he was or that anyone was even listening. I'd seen Spike close his eyes and play and then, when he finished, look really surprised to see me sitting there, listening. It was as if he was playing for himself and I just sort of happened to be around. Watching Troy, I could tell that he could be like that too — when he wasn't acting like his evil twin from another dimension, that is.

"Well, here goes," Troy suddenly said,

looking up and breaking into my thoughts.

Then he started playing. I leaned back and shut my eyes to hear the song better. Did you ever notice how if you close your eyes your hearing gets better or vice versa? I definitely think that I hear things much more clearly when I can't see.

Troy's song started out really upbeat, kind of catchy. But then there was this cool break — I could already hear a drum solo in it — and the song slowed way down. Then it ended on this long sad note that almost gave me the chills.

I kept my eyes closed for a few minutes after the music stopped. The last note had kind of lingered in the air before it died away. When I opened my eyes, Troy was looking at me expectantly.

"Well?" he said, sounding a little nervous. "Alton and Jim liked it, but . . . "

"I like it," I cut in before he could say anything else. "I really do. There's something sad about it, almost disturbing. It sort of leaves you with some questions that can't be answered."

Troy slowly started to smile. "You really think so?"

I nodded. "It's got soul," I declared.

"Didn't think I had in it me, did you?" Troy asked, laughing.

"Actually . . . " I began, not really knowing what I was going to say. Then I laughed out loud. He was right. I mean, even though I thought Iron Wombat had some kicking tunes, this was different. This song definitely pumped like their other stuff, but it had more depth. It was more than just a catchy tune.

"You know, I didn't either," Troy admitted with a flip of his hair. I suddenly noticed his eyes. They were really, really light brown . Looking at them right then, I didn't know how I could have missed how nice his eyes were.

"But you got me so mad, I knew I had to write something that would just blow you away," he continued. "It looks like it might have worked. What do you think?"

"You may be right," I admitted. I couldn't believe Troy had written this great song because he was mad at me. I mean, I know I drive some people to extremes — I admit it, I can be infuriating sometimes. But driving people to create . . . that was something else entirely. I wondered if I did that to my mother.

Just then, M came bursting through the front door. "Soup's on!" she called, putting the bags on the table. "I got some sweet and sour chicken too, so we wouldn't run out."

After we ate, M showed Troy all of her stuff — even her paintings from before. I didn't say too much for the rest of the night. I couldn't get Troy's tune out of my head.

For some strange reason, it reminded me of how I had felt when we moved out here from New York. I mean, Manhattan is so kicking all the time. Things can get kind of slow in Minnesota. At first, I had been afraid that I was going to fade out in Acorn Falls without all the excitement and action of New York around me. I had been so sure that without the hustle and bustle of New York I would change. I guess I did. But I didn't fade out. My perspective just changed, I suppose. Troy's music had really spoken to me. He obviously had no idea how he had touched me and I couldn't tell him in words. But he would by the time I was finished with those lyrics.

Chapter Eight

The band and I practiced really hard during the next two weeks. Soon it was the day before the Battle of the Bands. I decided to go skateboarding. For some reason I had a lot of excess energy. Everyday I found myself getting more keyed up about the whole thing. The guys loved my lyrics — even Troy and Iron Wombat sounded great, so it wasn't a worried kind of keyed up. Still I couldn't believe that we were actually going to play "Fade Out". That's what we all decided should be the name of Troy's song. Anyway, I couldn't believe that we were actually going to play the song in an auditorium full of people. It was a weird feeling — good but weird.

"Hey, watch it!" someone suddenly yelled as I swung onto Maple.

I looked up, and had the shock of my life!

"Sheck!" I screamed, totally shocked. "What ... who ... when ... "

"Hi ya, Ran!" Sheck replied, laughing at my surprise. "What's going on?" He grabbed me around the waist and swung me off my skateboard, giving me a major hug in the process.

As soon as Sheck set me down on the ground, I took a deep breath. I seriously could not believe Sheck was here — in Minnesota! What in the world was going on?

"I notice I have that affect on women," Sheck continued, grinning at me. "I leave them speechless."

"I can barely breathe with you standing so close to me," I answered in a breathy voice. "You make my heart skip a beat." Then I laughed.

It was kind of true, though I would never admit that to Sheck. You know how you have a picture in your mind of someone you care about who lives far away and then when you finally see him — especially when it's a shock — he's like larger than life. Sheck was definitely larger than life. And it wasn't the way he was dressed or anything. In fact, he kind of looked like he had just gotten out of bed. His long curly black hair was lying all flat on one side of his head as if he had slept on it. And he was wearing beat-up faded jeans, a really worn brown leather jacket and black oxford shoes. So why was my heart beating so fast — besides the fact that his eyes were the greenest ever?

Sheck laughed again. "So, Ran, surprised to see me?" he asked. Then he proceeded to get on my skateboard and jump off the curb onto the street.

"What are you doing here?" I finally asked.

"I was in the neighborhood?" Sheck suggested with a smile, flipping the skateboard up and catching it.

"Sheck. . ." I began, warningly.

"All right, all right," Sheck said, grabbing my hand and pulling me after him down the street. "I wanted to come and hear this happening new band I heard about. I've been told that they have this kicking tune, written by a slick new songwriter. They're making their debut tomorrow night and I didn't want to miss it."

I was glad that Sheck was walking a little bit ahead of me, because I suddenly felt like crying. I never cry. But I couldn't believe it. Sheck had come all the way from New York to hear my song!

Blinking furiously, I picked up my pace a little to keep up with him. "No, seriously," I said, still convinced that there had to be another reason for Sheck to be here.

He stopped and turned around to face me. "Seriously, Ran," he said softly. He reached up and touched my cheek. "That's why I'm here."

I didn't say anything — I couldn't. So I just stared into those incredible green eyes instead.

"Come on, R.Z.," Sheck suddenly said, breaking our gaze. He grabbed my hand and pulled me down the block again. "Olivia said we should pick up a good slice-and-dice horror flick at the video store. She's making pizza right now."

"She's making it?" I asked, surprised. M doesn't like to cook. Actually, that's not true. She just hates the time it takes to cook. And M can't stand cleaning up — she seriously trashes the kitchen.

"Yeah, we better hurry or the pizza will be burnt by the time we get back," Sheck replied, laughing. "You know how she is about forgetting to take things out of the oven."

I definitely did. Luckily, we made it home in

time. Sheck and I almost always agree on movies quickly. Right away we picked out *Twice Dead*, which is one of our favorites.

It's funny how it always takes forever for Sabs, Allison, Katie, and me to pick out a movie. Sabs usually wants to get some teenage romance, Katie wants a sports flick or a comedy, Allison wants something dramatic or serious and, of course, I want something warped. Once, it took us forty-five minutes to pick out one movie.

Anyway, Sheck and I managed to catch the pizza right before it burned. Then the three of us ate it and watched our movie. I wasn't really paying close attention, though. I kept looking over at Sheck, still in shock that he was actually there. I couldn't believe that he had come all that way just to hear my song.

After dinner I called Allison, Sabrina, and Katie to tell them Sheck had come all the way from New York to hear me play in the Battle of the Bands. I thought it was going to be a few quick phone calls, but I ended being on the phone for forty-five minutes! You wouldn't believe the shrieking and laughing that went on. On top of that, everyone had to say hi to

Sheck and ask a million questions.

Lying in bed that night, I couldn't fall asleep right away. It was weird. Even though I hadn't wanted to join Iron Wombat in the first place, the Battle of the Bands had suddenly become very important to me. And it wasn't only because Sheck was there.

The next morning I heard my mother moving around in the kitchen , so I got up to see what she was doing. "Is he still sleeping?" I asked M. "It's unreal how much he sleeps. We could make a movie about it, The Sleeping Dead, or something."

M laughed as she put the tea kettle on the stove. The two of us have herbal tea every morning. M is really into chamomile tea at the moment. She calls it the "wonder herb" and says everyone should have some every day. It doesn't taste too bad — especially with honey in it — so I don't mind going along with it.

I was sure Sheck would see it as yet another sign of my "countrification," though. He totally made fun of me the last time he was here. I think he thinks I'm turning into Becky HomeEcky or something. But I know now that you can take the girl out of the city, but you definitely can't take the city out of the girl.

"It's the age for sleeping late," M replied knowingly as she lined up three mugs by the stove. "Maybe some chamomile will help."Like I said, she's convinced that chamomile is the wonder herb.

"I think I'd better wake him," I said, moving toward the couch. "I've got practice in an hour."

"You know, Randy," M said, turning to face me. "I just wanted you to know that I'm really proud of you. Besides joining Iron Wombat, you've created something. You've written a song. Think about it. So many kids your age only care about going to the mall and hanging out. You, and your friends, do things — real things. And I just wanted you to know that I'm proud that you're able to be true to yourself and to your own creativity."

I just stood there for a second without saying anything. M usually doesn't go in for the traditional parent/kid talks. I walked over and gave her a big hug. "Thanks, M," I said softly, and then I jerked my head toward the sleeping lump on the couch. "And thanks for Sheck."

M laughed. "Oh, well that was really his

idea," she replied. "I just went to the airport to pick him up."

"Well, thanks anyway," I said and then marched quickly toward the living room area. "And now it's time to wake Sleeping Beauty." I chuckled my best evil death horror movie laugh and pounced on the sleeping lump on the couch. Sheck was awake in an instant.

"Hey!" Sheck yelled, putting up his arms to fight me off. He opened his eyes, moaned and shut them quickly. "What are you doing? It's still the middle of the night!"

"Good morning, Sunshine!" I said cheerfully and sat down on the floor. "I've got practice in an hour. "Sheck opened his eyes again more cautiously. "Really?" he asked. "Can I come, too?"

"Sure," I replied, surprised. It hadn't occurred to me that he might want to come to practice. But I decided as soon as he said it that it was a great idea.

"Do you have anyone working your board?" he asked, referring to the board that controls the sound levels and quality of each amp. Someone usually has to sit there when the band plays in order to make sure that no one instrument overpowers any of the others. You know how sometimes when a band plays you can barely hear the singer because the guitars are too loud? Well, that means that someone isn't working the board right. The singer's microphone should be turned up and the guitars toned down.

"You know," I replied, feeling a little foolish, "I'm not even sure if we have anyone to work the board at all. We haven't had anyone do it in practice. Jim usually deals with it before we start. But we'll definitely need someone on the board during the Battle of the Bands."

"Maybe I could do it," Sheck said, sitting up. "You know, Ran, you've really changed. You never used to get up before noon on weekends when you lived in the city. The country's changed you. I don't know if I like the new you."

"It's not so bad," I said, laughing. "Besides, somebody's got to milk the cows and water the crops."

"Water the crops?" Sheck repeated, standing up and wrapping his blanket more tightly around him. "Isn't that what rain's for?""Uh, right," I said, standing up and walking toward the kitchen. "What do you want for breakfast — hot or cold cereal, wheat flakes or oat bran?"

Sheck grumbled as he sat down at the table. "What kind of joint is this? What happened to steak and eggs?"

"Here's your tea," M announced, setting our mugs down on the table. "Morning, Sheck. How'd you sleep?"

"Like a rock, I'm sure," I said.

Looking at his mug as if it were filled with some kind of dangerous toxic waste or something, Sheck groaned again. "Don't let this happen to your kids," he said finally, staring at us across the table. "Make sure they get plenty of fried foods, sugar and caffeine every morning. Otherwise, their excessive cheerfulness may cause death."

M laughed. "I'd forgotten what a wry sense of humor you have, Sheck," she said, heading toward the bathroom.

"Who's joking?" Sheck asked as soon as the door had closed behind her.

"Come on, Sheckster," I said, putting a bowl of oat bran in front of him. "Get in gear. I don't want to be late." Sheck really has to have a fire lit under him in the mornings. He moves as if he were underwater, or something.

Forty-five minutes later, Sheck and I stood outside Troy's garage with my drums piled around us.

"Well, you want to help me set up this stuff?" I asked him, picking up one of the cases.

"If I must," Sheck said, with a heavy sigh. "I'm sure I'll be sore tomorrow, though. It looks really heavy."

I grinned at him. I had forgotten how much I missed being around him. Sabs, Al and Katie are great, they just don't the same kind of warped sense of humor.

"Hey, Ran!" Alton called out as he opened the garage door for me. "How are ya? Ready for tonight?"

I nodded. "I'm good to go," I announced. "Ready to rock the rafters. Oh, Alton, this is my friend Sheck," I said, introducing him. "He's from New York City."

"Cool," Alton remarked, shaking Sheck's hand. "What's up, dude? What are you doing in town?"

"Came to see this Battle of the Bands," Sheck said, following me to the back of the garage. "What do you guys win anyway?"

"I like that," Alton began, "he talks as if we've already won. We get a three weekend gig at Roadhouse." Sheck looked at us blankly and Alton went on to explain. "It's a new teen club out on Route 1, right next to the mall."

"Oh," Sheck replied.

"Well, we're as ready to rock as ever, right dude?" Alton continued, jerking his head toward Jim.

Jim nodded. I hadn't even noticed that he was there. Like I said — he hardly ever says a word.

"Well, let's jam," I said a few minutes later. "Where's Troy?"

"Oh, he's busy trying to arrange a van to take all our equipment over to the high school tonight," Alton explained, strapping on his guitar. "The dude's in the house with the phone attached to his ear."

I beat a sharp tatoo on my snare drum and then raised my stool a little. "Hey, do we have anyone working the board tonight?" I asked, suddenly remembering Sheck's offer.

Alton looked back at me, surprised. "No," he admitted. "I guess we thought Jim would just set all the levels before we played, the way he usually does."

Jim nodded again.

"Well," I began, tapping my cymbal a little to test the sound. "Sheck has offered to do it for us."

"Yeah?" Alton asked. "You can work a board?"

"Sure, no prob," Sheck replied, throwing himself down in an old padded chair. "You want me to do it now to get used to it?"

"Cool, man," Alton said, sorting through his box of picks. I have never seen such a collection of guitar picks in my life. When I asked him about it, Alton said that he chooses his pick according to his mood.

Sheck and Jim started checking out the board and began playing with the sound. Alton and I just jammed for a few minutes until the guys had set Alton's levels.

After a few minutes, Sheck came over to me, pushed me to one side of the stool and sat down. The stool was definitely not big enough for the two of us and I felt as if I was going to fall at any moment.

"Hey, Ran," Sheck said, grabbing one of my drumsticks. "Can we drum, like, tandem?"

"Sheck, you don't even know how to play," I pointed out.

"So?" he asked, putting his arm around my shoulders to keep me from sliding off the stool.

"Got a van!" Troy suddenly exclaimed, practically bursting into the garage. "My cousin. He'll be here at seven o'clock tonight."

"Great" said Alton, and he stopped playing.

Troy flipped his hair out of his eyes and suddenly glared at me. "Who's this?" he asked, gesturing to Sheck.

"Oh, that's Sheck," Alton said. "He's a friend of Randy's all the way from New York, and he's going to work our board tonight."

Sheck stood up and walked over to Troy. "How's it going, man?" Sheck said, holding out his hand.

Troy ignored it and glared at me. "Who decided he could work the board?"

Uh, oh. Troy Tanner's evil twin was back from the other dimension. I thought silently.

"We all did," Alton replied, sounding perplexed. "What's the big deal?"

"How do we know he can work a board?" Troy asked obnoxiously. "Why do we even need anyone working the board? Jim can do it, same as always."

"Troy," I began, trying to keep my temper. "I *know* Sheck can work a board. He's done it hundreds of times back at my old school in New York. Besides, you know as well as I do that having someone work the board while we play is the professional way to go."

Troy glared at me and gave his hair a flip. Then he turned and stared at Sheck, who, didn't even blink. I know for a fact that Sheck isn't afraid of anything, least of all, Troy Tanner.

"Well, I still don't think it's a good idea," Troy continued, not giving up.

"Well, I think he should work the board," Jim suddenly cut in, shutting everyone up. It was weird — the guy said so little that when he did talk, everyone listened.

"Really, Troy," I said, backing Sheck up. "What's the problem? Besides, you're not the whole band. And the three of us want him to work the board."

Troy's face began to turn red and he flipped his hair furiously. "I'm vetoing," he said, as if that settled the whole matter. Then he turned to Sheck. "Sorry, dude. This is a closed rehearsal."

That was it! I jumped up and stalked over to

where Troy was standing, calmly strapping on his guitar. I stopped when my face was only inches from his. "I don't know what your problem is," I began, practically yelling, "but I've had enough. What gives you the right to treat my friend — and us — like this? Who do you think you are anyway? Why don't you just chill out?"

Alton opened his mouth to say something, but Troy cut him off. "Listen, kid," Troy growled. I felt my hands form fists at my sides. "You just joined Iron Wombat a few weeks ago. So it's not as if you're like a full-fledged band member or anything."

"What?" I exploded in complete shock. "What do I have to do — go through an initiation? I wrote the song we're supposed to play tonight. I'm the drummer. What else do I have to do to become a member of Iron Wombat? Eat a goldfish?"

"I wrote that song," Troy contradicted, his brown eyes narrowing. "You just wrote the words."

"JUST?" I asked, completely furious. I was definitely beginning to see sparks. "Don't you mean that you just wrote the music."

"Which is really the song," Troy said.

What an incredible ego this guy had! It was a wonder he could get a guitar strap over his head, it was so inflated. That was it for me. He had gone too far this time.

"Well, you and your music can shove off!" I yelled. "I quit. Get your own words and find a new drummer! This scene is more than I can stomach!"

Whirling around, I practically ran smack into Sheck. "Let's go," I said to him and grabbed his hand.

"Randy, wait!" I heard Alton calling after us.

But no way was I waiting. Troy was really out of hand and I wasn't going to take it anymore. I knew I never should have joined their stupid band in the first place. It never would have worked out.

Chapter Nine

Alton calls Randy later that afternoon.

RANDY: Hello.

ALTON: Randy? This is Alton.

Randy doesn't answer.

ALTON: Listen, Randy . . .

RANDY: I quit, Alton. It's a final kind of thing. Don't bother trying to convince me to come back.

ALTON: Come on, Randy. The Battle of the Bands is tonight. You know Troy didn't mean all that stuff he was saying about "Fade Out." He's been telling you over and over how great the lyrics are.

RANDY: Right. That's why he said that I just wrote the words and that it was *his* song.

ALTON: Randy, you know how he is. He

	got a serious ego.
RANDY:	Well, I don't have to put up with it. I quit. He can go find another drummer.
ALTON:	Randy, you're not really being fair —
RANDY:	Fair? What are you talking about? Troy flips out on me, practically attacks my friend and then tells me that my song is not mine, and I'm not being fair?
ALTON:	Fine, Randy. Why don't you just quit, then? Good idea. I'm really glad that I went out on the limb for you when you tried out. If I had known you were going to quit so easily, I would've left you and your drums on Troy's front lawn three weeks ago. See ya, kid.

Sabrina calls Randy.

RANDY:	Hello.
SABRINA:	Ran, it's Sabrina. Tell me it's not true. It can't be possible. You didn't quit the band did you?
SABRINA:	I just saw Sheck in the video store. Gosh! is he gorgeous!

	Anyway, he told me that you and Troy had a big fight and you quit the band.
RANDY:	It's a fact, Sabs. I quit. And it was real easy. I just said, "I quit," and walked out.
SABRINA:	Well, what happened?
RANDY:	Sheck offered to work our control board, you know to control the sound and everything. Well, Troy said that Sheck couldn't work the board even though Alton, Jimmy, and I wanted him to. It was totally unreal. And then he said that I didn't write the song — that I had just done the words. That was it for me.
SABRINA:	Randy, what's Iron Wombat going to do now? They can't play tonight, can they?
RANDY:	Not without a drummer.
SABRINA:	Wow. that doesn't seem fair to Alton and Jimmy.
RANDY:	Sabs, you don't know what you're talking about, okay? You weren't there. Troy was way out

of line and I just couldn't put up
with it anymore.

SABRINA: Well, Luke knows Alton and he
told me that Alton was really
counting on that gig and that you
guys probably would have won.

RANDY: I can't help that, Sabs. Listen, I've
got to run. With Sheck visiting
and all, I've got a lot of things to
do around here, you know? I'll
see you Monday or something.
Ciao.

SABRINA: But Randy . . . listen, I think —
Never mind. See you.

Jim calls Randy.

RANDY: Hello.

JIM: Is this Randy?

RANDY: Yeah.

JIM: It's Jim. You know, from Iron
Wombat.

RANDY: I'm not coming back, Jim. I
already told Alton. I'll see you
around.

JIM: Wait a second, Randy. I know
you're pretty ticked off with Troy.

But the least you could do is listen to me for a minute.

There is a long pause.

RANDY: Okay.

JIM: Randy, why do you suppose Troy freaked today?

RANDY: I don't know. And I really don't care, all right?

JIM: I think you do. Otherwise, it wouldn't bother you at all.

RANDY: What? What do you mean?

JIM: Look, Randy. Lots of talented people have major attitudes. Troy definitely does, but so do you. So, when you and Troy get together, the sparks always fly. Sometimes it's not so cool, like today. Other times, it makes things happen. "Fade Out" is an incredible tune. You guys did that — together. You're obviously connecting on some level.

RANDY: Yeah, well tell that to Troy.

JIM: Did you ever stop to think that he just wasn't expecting Sheck. And that maybe he's a little jealous.

RANDY: WHAT?!

JIM: Just think about it, okay. And
           think about "Fade Out." You
           couldn't have done that with any-
           one else's music. And it wouldn't
           sound half as cool without your
           words. We need you, Randy. And
           you know, I think you need us,
           too.

There is another long pause.

RANDY: Okay. You're probably right about
           "Fade Out." But you can't expect
           me to believe that Troy is jealous
           of Sheck. He doesn't even know
           Sheck.

JIM: Well, I've known Troy a long
           time, Randy. Believe me, I know
           what I'm talking about. So, what
           do you say?

RANDY: All right, all right. But I'm not
           doing it for Troy. I'm doing it for
           Alton and you, okay?

JIM: And for yourself.

RANDY: Yeah, for myself. So, listen, why
           don't you guys bring the van by
           my place around seven-fifteen.

	Okay? We'll load up the drums and get to the the high school by seven-thirty.
JIM:	All right. See you in a few.
RANDY:	*Ciao.*

Randy calls Sabrina back.

SAM:	Wells'es residence. Sam here.
RANDY:	Hey, Sam. It's Randy. What's up?
SAM:	Randy! Is it true you're not play-ing tonight?
RANDY:	No, it's not true anymore. I'm playing. You will be there, won't you?
SAM:	Definitely!
RANDY:	Thanks. Is Sabs around?
SAM:	Yeah, I think she's up in her room, sulking or something. You wouldn't know anything about that, would you?
RANDY:	Would you just get Sabs for me, please.
SAM:	You sound just like Sabs, "It's none of your business, Sam."

Randy laughs.

| RANDY: | You sound just like Sabs. |

SAM: Yeah, well I've had lots of prac-
     tice. Hold on.

Sabrina comes to the phone.

SABRINA: Hello.

RANDY: Sabs, this is Randy.

SABRINA: Oh, hi.

RANDY: I don't blame you if you're mad.
     But I just wanted to call to tell
     you that you were right and I was
     wrong.

SABRINA: About what?

RANDY: It wasn't fair for me to quit Iron
     Wombat. I just got off the phone
     with Jim. He talked me into play-
     ing tonight. After that, we'll have
     to see.

SABRINA: You're really playing tonight?

RANDY: Yeah. And I'm sorry I was so
     obnoxious before.

SABRINA: That's okay, Randy. I knew you
     were just upset about Troy and
     everything. Hey, you said he
     started to get mad when he met
     Sheck. Do you think he's jealous
     or anything? I mean, it's pretty
     obvious that you and Sheck are

good friends . . .

RANDY: Sabs!

SABRINA: Well, it's true. At least, it's obvious to everyone else. Anyway, I bet that's what it was. Was Sheck standing near you when you introduced him? How'd you introduce him?

RANDY: Sheck was sitting on my drum stool with me and I didn't introduce him. Alton did. He said Sheck was my friend.

SABRINA: Well, there you go. Was Sheck holding your hand or something?

RANDY: He had one arm around me. Listen Sabs, you sound just like Jim. And I'll tell you the same thing I told him. I don't believe that Troy is jealous. It doesn't make any sense. I mean, Troy calls me kid. We fight all the time.

SABRINA: That's probably his way of hiding his feelings. Trust me, Ran. I know about these things.

RANDY Okay, okay. Listen, are you, Al, and Katie still going to come to the Battle of the Bands tonight?

SABRINA: Of course we are, Randy. Are you
ready to win?

RANDY: I'm ready to rock the roof off the
high school gym! We're going to
rock and roll until we drop.

SABRINA: All right! So, I'll see you there,
okay? Maybe we can go to Fitzie's
afterward or something.

RANDY: Definitely.

SABRINA: Great! See you later. 'Bye.

RANDY: *Ciao.*

Chapter Ten

A few hours before I was supposed to leave for the Battle of the Bands, I went upstairs to my room. M was in the studio working on one of her sculptures. Sheck had offered to make dinner. Believe it or not he's a great cook. I left him busy chopping ginger root in the kitchen. He muttered something about Thai cooking as he took out the wok.

When I lived in New York, he and I used to spend hours making masses of Thai food — the preparation takes forever, the cooking only moments. Then we'd invite hordes of friends over to eat. And there was always a ton left over.

I admit it. I was very keyed up. Cooking with Sheck would probably help me to relax, but I wasn't sure I wanted to relax. I play better

when I'm strung so tight I'm ready to twang —
like when I had tried out for Iron Wombat. The
tension had really got me going and I had
played well, if I do say so myself.

So, I wanted to stay kind of hyper. After I
got upstairs, I sat down at my drumset and
picked up my sticks. I didn't know what I felt
like playing, though. I knew I could plug my
headphones in and try to keep up with Buddy
Rich, but I wasn't really in the mood for that.

"Hey, Olivia!" I heard Sheck yell from
downstairs. "Do you mind if I put on some
music?"

"No problem," M replied after a long pause.
I stifled a giggle. That was so typical of M.
When she's into painting, it sometimes takes
her a little while to digest and answer questions.

A few moments later, the new tune by
Broken Arrow — my favorite New York band
— pumped out of our stereo downstairs. Sheck
had brought this tape with him. We had
listened to it pretty much non-stop since he had
gotten to Acorn Falls.

Suddenly, the adrenaline shot through my
veins. This was exactly what I needed. I would

keep the beat with Broken Arrow. Buddy Rich is awesome, but I needed something a little more on the cutting edge to warm up with tonight.

I smiled, telling myself I had to thank Sheck later. I knew he had put the record on for me. He really understood that I needed to hear it right then. A walkman would not have done it. Loud music was key.

Sometimes it can be scary when someone knows you that well. I didn't think that anyone would ever know me as well as he does here in Minnesota. Of course, that was before I met Allison, Sabs, and Katie.

After that tape ended, Sheck put on an awesome INXS tune called "Suicide Blond." I was really into the music and didn't even notice that M was standing in my doorway until the song was over. I wiped the sweat from my face and smiled at her.

"What's up, M?" I asked. "Is dinner ready so soon? Sheck usually takes forever to create his culinary masterpieces."

M laughed. "Yeah," she agreed, "but they're usually worth it." "I suppose you're right," I conceded. "Don't ever let him know I told you that. He's already got a major ego."

"Right," M joked. "And you've got a gentle soul. Sheck's fairly egoless, don't you think?"

I nodded. I just like to bust Sheck's chops, even when he's not around.

"No, to answer your original question," M said. "Dinner's not ready yet. You know how Thai is. I just came up to tell you that Allison, Katie, and Sabrina are here to wish you good luck. I know you're keyed up and I wasn't sure . . . ."

"Allison, Sabs, and Katie are here?" I asked, totally psyched. "Tell them to come on up."

M smiled and went back downstairs. A minute later, Sabs' head appeared at the top of the stairs.

"Close your eyes," she said breathlessly.

"What for?" I asked confused. I hate that sort of thing — you know, like when someone comes up from behind and puts their hands over my eyes and says "Guess who?"

"Close your eyes," Sabs repeated insistently. "We have a surprise for you."

"Sabs," I began warningly. She knows how I feel about closing my eyes. It's like I'm totally powerless or something.

"Just do it," Sabs begged. "Puh-lease."

Sighing, I closed my eyes. It's no use trying to argue with Sabrina when she's in a mood like this. Besides, I knew it must be important since she was pushing so hard. Suddenly, I heard Katie and Allison whispering as they walked slowly up the stairs. There was a loud clunking noise, then some giggles. Then I heard one of them run down the stairs, and a moment later, run back up again.

"Okay," Sabs said, her voice full of excitement. "You can open your eyes now."

"What are you guys doing anyway? Rearranging my furniture?" I asked as I opened my eyes. Katie, Al, and Sabs were all standing in front of me holding up huge posters with "Iron Wombat is Number 1!" written on them in big, bright letters. I didn't know what to say. It's not often that I'm left speechless, but I was. My friends were really, totally, incredibly cool.

"Do you like them?" Sabs questioned eagerly. "Allison and Katie did the lettering and I picked the colors."

"We're going to be your cheering section at the Battle of the Bands," Katie added with a grin.

"They're not really finished yet," Allison put in apologetically. "We still have to put the glitter on. But we bought a bottle of glitter with us and we'll finish before you go on stage."

"They look awesome, guys!" I exclaimed, finally finding my voice. I grinned at my friends. "Thanks."

"There's more," Sabs announced, practically throwing her poster on my bed and pointing to the top of the stairs.

Somehow, they had carried a dress dummy up the stairs to my loft. "So that's what all the noise was," I said with a laugh. Draped over the dummy was a jeans jacket I could have sworn belonged to Katie. "You brought me Katie's jean jacket?"

"Turn it around, Al," Katie directed. Allison quickly turned the dress dummy around.

"Do you like it?" Sabs asked immediately.

"How did you do it?" I asked, walking closer to look at Katie's jacket. Somehow, they had printed the band name on the back in bright red letters, outlined with black and silver.

"My sister has a silk screening kit," Katie explained. "We designed it and she helped us make them. We each have one."

"Jim and Alton'll flip when they see these," I exclaimed. "We'll be the only band there with a fan club!"

"If you want, we can make T-shirts and stuff for the band," Al offered. "We still have the screen and everything."

"Oh no!" Sabs exclaimed suddenly. "I forgot to tell my brother to bring the tickets when he picks us up here to take us to the high school tonight. Can I use your phone?"

"Sure," I said, pointing to the phone on the floor. "I brought it up here because Sheck complained that the ringing destroyed his beauty sleep," I added with a laugh.

"You know, it's so cool that Sheck came all the way to Minnesota to watch you in the Battle of the Bands!" Sabs exclaimed as she picked up the phone.

While Sabs called her brother, Allison and Katie put the finishing touches on the jackets and posters. Then Sheck called up the stairs inviting everybody to join in the feast. I felt pretty warmed up at this point, but they all wanted to hear me play before we ate so I sat back down behind my drums and banged out a few songs. After Sheck's tape stopped, we all flopped on my bed. I was still keyed up, but in a really positive way.

"I've got to take a shower," I announced, not making any movement. "I'm moving now. Can you see me? I'm getting in the shower as we speak."

Sabs giggled. "Get in gear!" she said, sounding like me. "It smells as if Sheck's cooking now. He had all these things cut up in bowls all over the kitchen. He said he was making tie food. What's that anyway? Food you have to tie or something? And what was he going to do with that coconut?"

"It's Thai food," I said, stifling a giggle. "T-H-A-I. From Thailand."

"Oh," Sabs said, blushing a little.

"Yo, chickies!" Sheck called from downstairs. "Soup's on!"

We looked at each other and giggled. Talk about speaking of the devil.

I stood up and grabbed a sweatshirt. "I guess I'll have to shower after dinner," I said, turning toward the stairs. "Hey!" I called back to Sheck. "We are not little birds! You got that!"

"Hey, haven't you heard of the First Amendment?" Sheck asked, as we all trooped into the kitchen. "Freedom of speech and all that."

"Yeah, yeah," I agreed, looking around the kitchen. Steaming bowls of food were on every available surface. "Thai Death! This looks awesome."

"Thanks," Sheck replied, bowing from the waist. "Call me Mr. Dalai — Thai chef extraordinaire."

He handed everyone a bowl of something and sent us over to the table. Sheck followed with two pitchers of water.

"Olivia!" Sheck called out, sitting down. "Time to eat. Don't forget to wash your hands!"

M walked over to the table and held up her hands for inspection. "Now, I know your mother doesn't say that. Wherever did you learn it from?" she asked, laughing.

"June Cleaver," he replied, picking up a bowl of orange noodles. "Now, we're going to start off with Pad Thai."

"Pad what?" Katie asked.

"Pad Thai," I replied. "Rice noodles, really. They're great."

"Hey, where's the silverware?" Sabs asked.

"We only use chopsticks," Sheck said. "It's a

Thai Death tradition. We're not wusses. We're men."

I cleared my throat loudly.

"I mean, we're people."

Everyone picked up their chopsticks and tried to hold them. I was prepared to help Sabs, who was sitting next to me, but she totally surprised me.

"Sabs, how do you do that?" Katie asked, as Sabs served Pad Thai onto her plate with her chopsticks. She picked up a few stray noodles quite deftly.

"No problem," Sabs said, grinning. "I used to use chopsticks a lot when I was little. And then I read something about all these actresses eating Sushi out in L.A. Not that I would ever eat raw fish. That's totally disgusting. But, you know, when I get famous, I might have to eat in restaurants like that. Even if it is only rice. I wouldn't want to be the only one using a fork. So I've been practicing. Sam is always making fun of me, of course."

"So, how do you hold them?" Katie asked, when Sabs took a breath.

"Well," Sabs began. She loves to teach people how to do things. "Hold one stick in your hand like you do a pencil. That chopstick doesn't move. The other one you hold on top of the first, and your pointer finger moves it. That's the only stick that moves."

For a few minutes, Allison and Katie tried to pick up their napkins with their chopsticks.

"Okay, kids," Sheck said, interrupting their lesson. "Let's get our plates filled and chow!" He began passing around the rest of the bowls.

"What's this?" Allison asked, holding up a bowl.

"Nue Qua Poa," Sheck replied. "Beef with mint. Make sure you fill up your water glass before eating that. It's extremely hot. Major chilis in it."

"And what's this?" Sabs asked.

"Panang Nue," I said. "Coconut milk and beef. It's pretty hot. Not terrible, though."

"This is great!" Katie exclaimed. Then she gasped and reached for her glass of water. "Oh my gosh! My mouth is burning up."

Sheck and I looked at each other and started laughing. That is exactly why we love it, because it's so hot.

We all stuffed ourselves for twenty minutes. And then M brought out the cake. Chocolate fudge layer cake — my favorite.

"Can we use forks for this?" Katie asked, massaging her hand. "My fingers are killing me."

M laughed. "Sure, Katie," she said, cutting the cake.

Finally, we were all finished eating. That meal was just what I had needed to get my blood moving. Not that I wasn't wired before. Jumping up, I started picking up the plates.

"Leave it, hon," M said, taking the plates from me. "I'll get them."

I must have looked really shocked. M never washes dishes. She'd rather throw them out first.

M laughed. "I'm sure my hands won't fall off," she joked. "Get in the shower. Aren't the guys from the band going to be here in less than forty-five minutes?"

Suddenly, someone honked outside. "That's my brother!" Sabs exclaimed. "We'd better get going. You know how Luke hates to wait." She rolled her eyes at all of us. I do know. Sabs's older brother, Luke, just got his license. Part of the deal for him getting to use the family car is driving Sabs and Sam around. It is just about like the last thing he wants to do. So he has all these rules when we ride with him — like no talking to him unless he speaks first, and no playing with the radio. He is a real auto tyrant.

"We'll see you over there, Randy," Allison said, grabbing her coat and walking toward the door. "I know you'll do great."

"How are you feeling?" Katie asked, following Al.

"I'm ready to jam" I exclaimed, bouncing around a little. And I was. I was totally good to go! Acorn Falls wouldn't know what hit it after Iron Wombat was finished.

I just hoped the rest of the band was as up for this as I was.

Chapter Eleven

"Are you ready to rock and roll?" Mike McCray, the M.C., screamed at eight o'clock that night to a packed auditorium. "Are you ready to dance till you drop? Party till you pop?" Mike is a deejay at WXKG, the radio station that was sponsoring the Battle of the Bands.

The crowd roared its answer.

"Sounds like there's a lot of people out there," Alton said, sorting through his box of guitar picks. "How many people do you think they can fit in this auditorium anyway?"

"Does it matter?" Jim asked, raising his eyebrows at me.

"I guess not," Alton answered, choosing a tortoise-shell pick and shutting the box. "I just wondered."

Then Mike introduced all the judges. There was the station programmer from WXKG, a

111

man who owned a record store in the mall, a record producer from Minneapolis who was the aunt of an Acorn Falls High student, and a singer from the area who was supposedly on the verge of making it. I don't know who I had expected the judges to be, but at least they were in the music industry and not like the principal and school nurse or something.

Just then, Escape, the first band, was introduced. As they finished setting up their equipment, Alton and Jim started talking about how they weren't too impressed with Escape's song selection — something by Motley Crue.

"You know, Randy," Sheck said, pulling me off to the side. "I'm glad you decided to go through with this. I mean, Tanner seems like sort of a jerk, but these other two guys are cool. Anyway, lots of really talented musicians are moody."

I shrugged. I had really never thought about what musicians might be like as people.

"You know, R.Z., you're going to rock the house," Sheck continued confidently. "Record deals will start pouring in. You'll go on the road, have to get a tutor, hit the covers of all the big mags. You know, you'll probably call me a lot in the beginning. But as you get more famous, the calls will taper off. Then there will be just a scribbled postcard from a faraway place once every four or five weeks. Finally, we'll be reduced to Christmas cards — and yours will be written in your agent's handwriting." He paused and wiped an imaginary tear from his very green eyes. "It's been nice knowing you, Randy."

I laughed. Sheck is such a goof. He really is. Not to mention the fact that he looked great in the black turtleneck and faded black jeans he was wearing. Black is really a great color on him. It makes his eyes look even more green, if that is possible.

Of course, black is my favorite color, too. I was wearing a black sleeveless mini-dress, with black-and-white tie-dyed tights, and black oxford shoes. Even though it was still winter and cold outside, I can't drum in sleeves. They get in my way and slow me down.

"Hey, Sheck," I said softly, turning serious. I reached over and gave him a hug. "Thanks a lot for coming out. I really appreciate it. And thanks for helping us out."

Sheck hugged me tightly for a moment, not

letting me go. "It's no big deal, Ran," he said into my ear. "Besides, I didn't want you to forget what I look like."

Like that was even possible. Sheck's mother is a photographer and he's practically her favorite subject. Of course, he sends me boatloads of pictures of him.

"Uh, Randy, could I talk to you for a second," Troy suddenly cut in from somewhere behind me. Sheck let me go and turned around to look at Troy. "You mind if I talk to her alone," Troy added, looking back at Sheck.

"Go ahead," Sheck said, walking away. "I've got to discuss feedback with Jim."

After Sheck had gone, Troy didn't say anything for a minute or so. He just started at my shoes and flipped his hair, nervously.

Finally he cleared his throat. "Uh, Randy," he began, "I just want to tell you that I'm glad you showed up tonight. I was really off-base earlier and I wouldn't have blamed you if you had just canned the whole thing."

I didn't say anything. The evil twin must have been banished to the other dimension again. The nice Troy Tanner was back.

"Anyway, I'm sorry," he continued, finally

looking up at me. He stared at me for a second and then cleared his throat. "And I hope you stay in Iron Wombat. You're a great drummer and your song is definitely cool."

"Thanks," I said. I knew it must have been hard for him to apologize to me. But it was probably even harder for him to refer to our song as my song.

"And uh . . . I was . . . wondering if . . . " he stuttered. "Maybe we could catch a movie sometime. You know, after this Battle of the Band stuff is over." Troy flipped his hair and smiled.

My mouth dropped open. I couldn't believe it. Maybe Sabs and Jim were right. Maybe Troy was jealous of Sheck. I was definitely at a loss for words, which doesn't happen often. I always have a comeback ready.

"We'll see," I finally said. It was kind of a lame response, but it was the best I could do under the circumstances.

"Well think about it anyway," Troy replied, sounding pleased. "Hey, did you check out the audience?" he asked, changing the subject. "You can look out from behind the curtain between bands."

That was cool. If I could find out where Sabs, Al and Katie were sitting then I wouldn't have to look for them when we hit the stage.

"Those guys were dogs!" Alton exclaimed as Escape left the stage. "I really think you've got to have long hair and tatoos if you're going to play heavy metal. Those preps just didn't have it, you know?"

I laughed. I couldn't agree more. Escape just didn't have the proper image. Not that image really has that much to do with music, but Escape didn't have the talent either.

"When do we go on?" I asked, suddenly realizing that we could be next for all I knew.

"They're saving the best for last," Alton replied, pulling on a black blazer over the white shirt that he had buttoned all the way up to his neck. No tie. I have to say this for Alton, he definitely has style. He looks like a young Denzel Washington — pretty hot.

"We're last?" I asked in surprise. Last was a great spot. No one would follow us and make our performance fade at all. I wondered how we gotten a spot like that.

"Great, isn't it," Troy said, flipping his hair. "And it was just luck of the draw. Incredible."

"Sure it was," Alton shot back, laughing. "It had absolutely nothing to do with the fact that you did an internship at WXKG last semester, right?"

Troy grinned back. "Right," he said, taking his guitar out of the case and strapping it on.

Escape finally got it's equipment off the stage and the next band, an all-girl group called Lucky Ladies, started setting up their mikes. It was a really good thing that Mike, the M.C., was such a funny guy. Otherwise the people in the audience would have gotten bored out of their gourds between bands.

I walked over to the curtain and peeked out at the crowd. The house lights were half-lit so I could still see people's faces.

"Randy!" I suddenly heard Sabs scream. "Over here!" I saw Sabs on the right-hand side of the middle section. Al and Katie were sitting next to her. Sabs was jumping up and down in her seat, waving at me. I caught her eye and she smiled, opening her eyes really wide. Then I saw Spike sitting right next to her. I grinned and winked. I knew Sabs was clearly in seventh heaven.

Katie and Allison gave me the thumbs-up

sign and I gave one back to them. I looked next to Al and there was M. She had the biggest smile of everyone. Suddenly she blew me a kiss. Cool! Once I saw M I knew everything was going to be great.

I was just about to wave to M again when I felt someone tap me on the shoulder. I spun around and saw Sheck standing right behind me. He grinned.

"So, R.Z.," he began, trying so hard to sound casual that he sounded anything but. "Did you get a date with the handsome and talented Troy Tanner?" he asked, not meeting my eyes.

I thought he was joking again and I was about to laugh. But I took one look at Sheck's face and realized he was being serious about this and he wasn't trying to hide it anymore.

"Sheck, he asked me to a movie," I began, and then paused. "But you know I'm just not into the couple thing. The whole dating scene is not for me, you know?" I continued, trying to make him understand.

Sheck's face split into a wide smile. "So you turned him down?"

"Not exactly," I hedged. "But if I do decide

to go to a movie with him, it doesn't have anything to do with how I feel about you."

"Oh," Sheck replied a little sulkily.

"C'mon Sheckster, don't worry," I said, laughing. "You're number one. Besides, I don't like to mix business with pleasure. I'm not sure I want to go out with someone in my own band."

"You're going to stay in Iron Wombat?" Sheck asked in surprise. "I thought you were just coming back for tonight."

"You're not going to leave?" Alton suddenly asked, coming up behind us. "All right!"

"Yeah, you've got too much style for me to leave you alone with those clowns," I said, laughing at Alton's enthusiasm. Alton grabbed the lapels of his jacket and turned to look at Jim's plain old white T-shirt and jeans.

"Dude!" Alton exclaimed as Troy walked over to us. "You look ready to rock." I admit Troy did look good. He had on black pleated pants, a white T-shirt and a black vest.

"Let's go!" Troy said, grabbing his guitar. "We're up next."

We were next? How had that happened? I had completely lost track of time. In fact, I barely remembered any of the other bands after the first two. I licked my lips and gave myself a mental shake. I was ready for this. I really was. Before I knew it, Mike had introduced us. The place went wild. It was pretty obvious from the applause that Iron Wombat had a good reputation in Acorn Falls. I waved at my fans — Sabs, Al, Katie, M and Spike — and I sat down at my drums.

"Let's go, Ran," Sheck called out from the wings where he was sitting with the board. I glanced at him and he winked back

Troy turned around and raised his eyebrows at me. "Ready?" he asked the band in general.

Alton and Jim nodded. "Let's rock the house!" I exclaimed, starting the staccato beat introduction to "Fade Out."

Troy spun toward the mike and picked up the rhythm on his guitar. He started to sing and my words filled the auditorium.

It seemed like we had just started, when the last notes to "Fade Out" died away. The silence was deafening when we stopped. Then suddenly, the whole place erupted. Pandemonium is the key phrase here. I grinned. We must have seriously rocked.

I saw Sabs, Al and Katie jumping up and down screaming. Then I noticed M. She looked as if she was crying! Suddenly, Sheck practically knocked me off my stool as he raced over to give me a hug.

"You rocked, girl!" he practically screamed in my ear. Then Jimmy, Alton, Troy and I rushed off stage.

A few minutes later M.C. Mike announced that Iron Wombat was the winner of the Battle of the Bands!

I glanced back at Sheck, then I looked over at Sabs, Katie and Al, and M. I suddenly realized that it wouldn't have mattered if Iron Wombat had won or lost. We had done it — I had done it! And that was all that really mattered.

Titles in the GIRL TALK series

1 WELCOME TO JUNIOR HIGH!
Introducing the Girl Talk characters, Sabrina Wells, Katie Campbell, Randy Zak, and Allison Cloud. When our four heroines meet and have to plan the first junior high dance of the year, the results are hilarious.

2 FACE-OFF!
Katie Campbell is just plain fed up with being "perfect." But when she decides to join the boys' ice hockey team, she gets more than she bargained for.

3 THE NEW YOU
Allison Cloud is down in the dumps, and her friends decide she needs a makeover, just in time for a real live magazine shoot!

4 REBEL, REBEL
Randy Zak is acting even stranger than usual — could a visit from her cute friend from New York have something to do with it?

5 IT'S ALL IN THE STARS
Sabrina Wells's twin brother, Sam, enlists the aid of the class nerd, Winslow, to play a practical joke on her. The problem is, Winslow takes it seriously!

6 THE GHOST OF EAGLE MOUNTAIN
The girls go camping, only to discover that they're sleeping on the very spot where the Ghost of Eagle Mountain wanders!

LOOK FOR THE GIRL TALK SERIES!
COMING SOON TO A STORE NEAR YOU!

TALK BACK!

TELL US WHAT YOU THINK ABOUT GIRL TALK

Name _____

Address _____

City _____ State _____ Zip _____

Birthday: Day _____ Mo _____ Year _____

Telephone Number (____) _____

1) On a scale of 1 (The Pits) to 5 (The Max),
how would you rate Girl Talk?   Circle One:

          1   2   3   4   5

2) What do you like most about Girl Talk?

___Characters___Situations___Telephone Talk

Other _____

3) Who is your favorite character?   Circle One:

    Sabrina   Katie   Randy

    Allison   Stacy   Other

4) Who is your least favorite character?

_____

5) What do you want to read about in Girl Talk?

_____

_____

Send completed form to :
Western Publishing Company, Inc.
1220 Mound Avenue Mail Station #85
Racine, Wisconsin 53404